SLIMCONSIN

DONT

$ $

The Trenches

Murder, Money, Betrayal

Kutta

The Trenches

Murder, Money, Betrayal

Printed in the United States of America.

ISBN: 978-1-7366158-0-5

Table of Contents

Chapter One

* * * * *

It was 11:35pm on a Friday night and Scooter sat in his mother's car outside of his best friend Keef's house. He was looking down at his phone as he waited on Keef and his twin brother, Keimon, to come outside. Scooter heard a loud bang on his passenger side window that startled him, causing him to fumble and drop his phone. He looked up, and quickly unlocked the door after noticing it was Keef banging on the window. "Nigga, why the fuck you banging on the window like that?" Scooter asked. "Don't get mad at me 'cause I scared yo bitch ass!" Keef said as he laughed and got into the passenger seat and stuffed his book bag in between his legs. Keimon quickly jumped in the back seat and closed the door as he laughed. Scooter looked back at Keimon, "I know you ain't laughing nigga, you scared to get the pussy from Lisa!" Scooter said before he and Keef both started laughing. "Nigga, I ain't scared of shit, definitely not Lisa. I just didn't want to fuck that bitch, that's all" Keimon said as he looked away from Scooter and started staring out the window. "Yeah, light that's what you said about Toya too!" Scooter said as he turned back around and picked up his phone. "Bro, I wanna fuck that bitch Toya bad! You gotta get that lil pussy and tell me if it's good or not" Keef said in a real calm tone. "Man, fuck that bitch, we on this money tonight. Did y'all bring the heat?" Scooter quickly asked. "Nigga, you know I stay strapped! This bet not be a sendoff mission like that last one we went on" Keef said. "Hell, yeah 'cause we only got two hunnit a piece off that shit!" Keimon quickly added. "That was a whole lot better than what you broke ass niggas had before I called y'all" Scooter said as he pulled off. "But on some real shit, this mission gone have us straight for a while. Y'all remember that Arabian nigga y'all was talking shit about me hanging wit last week?" Scooter asked. "Yeah, I remember that nigga." Keef responded. "Well, that nigga pops owns that liquor store over there on University. I went to the nigga's crib the other day, and when I say them bitches rich my nigga, I mean it, they rich! The nigga showed me three hunnit Gs in a chest in his basement. The nigga said it was petty cash they use to buy shit day to day. He gave me five hunnit like it wasn't shit. But long story short, I been sticking to his hip so I can figure out what's the best time to slide in his crib and get that shit. He told me they going to Chicago to visit his uncle for the weekend, so tonight is the night we going in that bitch!" Scooter said. "You sure they gone?" Keef curiously asked wanting to make sure Scooter was right. "On my life! I been on his hip all week, nigga! Trust me the money there and they gone! Y'all niggas wit it or not?" Scooter asked as he began to grow a little frustrated with Keef and Keimon not believing this was a legit mission. Keef and Keimon both sat there quiet as Scooter continued to drive down Whitney Way. "Ight, fuck it, I'm wit it!" Keef said as he rubbed his hands together in anticipation of what was to come. Keef was the oldest and the leader of the group, so whatever he was with his younger brother, Keimon, was with it too.

Without saying a word, Keimon nodded his head letting Scooter know he was with it too. "Ight, look, when we pull up make sure y'all niggas ready. Whatever we get, we gone bust it down three ways and none of that stashing shit either!" Scooter said as he looked in his rearview mirror at Keimon then turned onto University Avenue. "Nigga, I don't know why you looked back here when you said that shit!" Keimon said. "'Cause that's what you be on, nigga!" Keef said as he reached down and turned the music up then sat back as Drake's song "Successful" poured from the speakers. Keimon sat in the back seat nervous he wasn't sure how this was going to turn out. He didn't trust Scooter's word after the last mission they went on, but was going along with the ride anyway. Scooter turned onto Shorewood Hills and drove up the block, then pulled over and parked two houses from the corner. "Look, it's that house right there" Scooter said as he hit the lights and pointed to a big stone house on the corner. Keimon's heart dropped to his stomach as he looked at the big stone house. "That's a big ass house, nigga, you sure they gone?" he asked. "Yeah, nigga! You see all the lights out" Scooter instantly replied. "Bro, that don't mean shit!" Keef added. "You bitch ass niggas can just give me the heat and look out! When I come out with this bag, Imma give y'all niggas five Gs to split." Scooter said as he looked at Keef with a real devilish look in his eyes. Keef could tell by the look on his face Scooter was serious about the cash really being in that house. "Hell naw, nigga, I ain't firma sit in the car! We here now let's go!" Keef said as he unzipped his book bag and pulled out a 9mm and a ski mask and handed it to Scooter. "Ight, then let's get paid!" Scooter said as Keef passed another 9mm and a ski mask to Keimon. "Y'all niggas wait right here. I'm finna go in through the window. When y'all see the front door open, hurry up and come in, I don't want these rich ass white people to see three niggas outside." Scooter said as he pulled his ski mask over his face, pulled his hood over his head and got out of the car.

Keef and Keimon both sat there and watched as Scooter quickly ran around to the back of the house. "Bro, if this nigga know where the money at, why he don't just go get it? Fuck he need us to come in for? I don't trust this nigga!" Keimon said as they both watched for the front door to open. "He good, bro. He need us just in case it's somebody in the house. You tripping, bro, just relax!" Keef said. Just as Keef finished his sentence, the front door opened up and Scooter waved them in. "Come on!" Keef said as he jumped out the car and hurried to the house. Keimon wasted no time getting out the car and was steps behind his brother. A bad feeling instantly overcame Keimon as he stepped into the huge house and closed the door. "Find what you can on this floor" Scooter whispered to Keef. "You check upstairs and Imma hit the basement for the bread in the chest" Scooter whispered to Keimon. Keef went straight to work as Scooter rushed towards the basement. Keimon slowly walked to the stairs and his palms began to sweat. His heart pounded a thousand beats per second as he walked up the stairs. *Why the fuck these bitch ass niggas send me upstairs*? he thought to himself as he made it to the top of the staircase. He crept down the hall and slowly pushed open the first door on his right and peeked in noticing the room was completely empty. He closed the door and continued to walk down the dark hall. He noticed another door on his left, and slowly walked to it and pushed it open. "Damn, this a big ass office" he thought to himself as he walked in and scanned for a sign that no one was there. "Yeah, these bitches rich!" He said out loud as he rushed over to the desk in the middle of the huge room. Keimon rummaged through every drawer looking for anything of value he could find.

"OH SHIT!" he shouted aloud as his bones almost jumped out of his skin and took off running when he noticed someone was hiding under the desk. "Please, please, don't hurt me!" a small frail woman said as she tried to scoot further under the desk. Keimon reached under the desk and pulled her up to her feet. "Bitch, you called the police?" He asked as he snatched the cell phone from her hand and threw it on the floor. "Please, don't hurt me! Take what you want! Please! please, listen! There's nine million dollars' worth of diamonds in the safe behind that picture on the wall, just take it and go! The police are on the way!" She said as she pointed to a huge portrait of herself on the wall across the room. "Okay, well bitch, let's open it and find out!" Keimon said as he grabbed a fistful of her hair and pushed her across the room. "Bitch, hurry up and open it!" he said as he pointed his pistol at her, the small woman quickly snatched the picture from the wall and started spinning the dial on the safe. The woman trembled in fear, her hands began to shake as she fumbled with opening the safe. "Bitch, you better hurry up! If you keep stalling, Imma just shoot yo ass in the back of yo head and leave!" Keimon whispered as he pressed his pistol firmly against the back of her head. "Please don't! It's, it's almost open!" the woman stuttered as she pulled the lever down and pulled open the safe. Keimon shoved her to the side and looked in the safe and seen a bunch of paper bonds and a small black bag. Knowing time wasn't on his side, he grabbed the black bag and opened it. His eyes lit up at the site. He had never seen so many diamonds in his life. He closed the bag and stuffed it into his pocket. "Now, bitch, lay face down on the floor and count to a thousand before you get up!" He said to the woman as he pushed her to the floor. She immediately started counting "One, two, three, four..." Keimon rushed out of the room and ran down the hall. "The police coming! The police coming!" Keimon yelled out to Scooter and Keef as he stumbled down the stairs. "What?" Scooter asked as he came up from the basement with a black trash bag in his hand. "It's a bitch upstairs and she called the police, we gotta go! We gotta go!" Keimon shouted as he ran towards the door. "I got the money! We gone! Let's go!" Scooter shouted to Keef. Keef heard the shouting as he searched the downstairs office and panicked. He dropped the Rolex watch he found and ran out of the room. Speeding through the kitchen, he slipped and fell, causing him to slide across the marble floor. He quickly jumped back up to his feet and ran towards the door where Scooter stood waiting on him. They both bolted through the door and rushed to the car.

Scooter tossed the bag in the back seat with Keimon as he closed his door and started the car. Keef was steps behind Scooter as he jumped into the car. Scooter put the car into drive and sped off. "What y'all get?" Scooter asked Keef and

Keimon as he turned onto University Avenue. "Shit!" Keef said as he looked around to see which direction the sirens were coming from. "Man, that bitch scared the shit out of me! Nigga, you said they was gone!" Keimon shouted at Scooter. "Nigga, I didn't know the bitch was gone be there!" he said as he sped down University Avenue. "Fuck, they on us!" Scooter shouted out. "Damn!" Keef said as he looked back and seen that the police were about half a block behind them. "They got us fucked! I ain't going to jail!" Keef said as he rolled his window down and cocked his pistol. Scooter hurried and made a right turn onto Midvale Boulevard, and stomped on the pedal, pushing it to the floor as they flew past the Hillsdale Mall at a 100 mph. "Bro, we can't get caught with that bread! I'm finna bend a corner, y'all niggas hurry up and jump out" Scooter said as he looked in his rearview mirror. "Bro, I ain't finna leave you! Keimon, grab that bread and jump out as soon as we hit this corner." Keef said. "Ight" Keimon said without hesitation before grabbing the bag and looking back to see how far back the police was. Scooter swerved from lane to lane as the tires screeched and he battled for control of the car. He made a right turn onto Merlham Road at 50, then completely lost control of the car, running directly into a tree. Keimon was tossed off impact from the back seat. He landed in between the passenger and the driver's seat. He instantly panicked when he looked over and seen Scooter laid up against the steering wheel bleeding from his head. He wiped the pieces of glass off his shoulder as he looked to the passenger seat, then to the big hole in the front windshield realizing his brother was nowhere in sight. "What the fuck!" Keimon shouted. He climbed from in between the seats into the backseat then hopped out of the car. "Keef! Keef, bro, where you at?" Keimon cried out. Smoke filled the air from the mangled piece of metal that was once Scooter's mother's prized possession. Keimon looked around for Keef, but noticed the red and blue lights reflecting off the nearby buildings on Midvale Boulevard. Keimon looked back and knew within seconds the police would be turning that corner. Without hesitation, he rushed back to the car, grabbed the bag of money, and took off running into the darkness of the night.

Chapter Two

* * * * *

A s Vito stared out the window at the trees from his six by nine-foot cell, he couldn't help but reflect back on his life. After serving a five-year bid in Federal prison, he'd only had a year run before he was back in again. This time serving a life sentence. Going back to 2004, when he was released from Federal prison, he hit the ground running. The very moment he stepped foot back on 21st & Scott he was met with open arms by his SD brothers. Vito stood tall and took the time for his best friend Carlos, so it was only right that Carlos put him back on top. Standing only 5'5", Vito was well-known throughout the streets of Milwaukee, Wisconsin for being a bricklayer with the heart of a lion. Carlos was also known for getting money, but relied on Vito and the SDs for his protection.

"Welcome home!" Carlos said as he shook Vito's hand and pulled him in for a hug. "It's good to be home!" Vito responded while embracing Carlos. "I see you looking like money!" Vito quickly added as he broke away from Carlos' grip and looked at his attire. "You know, I do me" Carlos said as he looked Vito in his eyes. "Well, I'm back, baby! Get me together!" Vito said before he turned and looked back at the rest of his friends. "Let's take a ride!" Carlos said as he put his arm around Vito's shoulder and walked him to his Mercedes. The moment Vito and Carlos were out of ear shot of everyone else, Carlos filled Vito in on his business operations.

Carlos had evolved greatly during the five years Vito was in prison, he owned multiple businesses and real estate properties across Milwaukee. Carlos was no longer hands-on in the coke game, but he was still knee deep in it with workers all throughout the city. Now that Vito was home, Carlos knew it was time to let Vito have his way in the streets so he could get his money together. Carlos wasted no time rolling out the red carpet for Vito. Vito took full advantage of the opportunity and immediately started laying down his groundwork and making his presence felt again. In a matter of months, Vito had the city in a chokehold and was having his way. He linked with a few niggas out East, where the real money was, and opened up a few spots. For six months straight, Vito stood ten toes down and did nothing but hustle.

One morning, Vito felt like he needed to take some time and enjoy being free, so he called up Carlos and Dro to get away from Milwaukee for a while. Carlos knew all the establishments where it would be popping, he wanted to show Vito a good time, so they hit up the Hideaway strip club in Rockford, Illinois. The Hideaway was packed from wall to wall as money fell from above onto the strippers. Vito, Carlos, and Dro stood on the couches on the upper level surrounded by strippers when Vito noticed a female across the room delivering bottles to a group of black guys. Vito tapped Carlos on his shoulder and pulled him closer. "Aye, do you know shorty over there? " Vito asked as he pointed across the room. "You talking about shorty in the red?" Carlos asked confused. "Naw, the short one with the fat ass standing next to her." Vito quickly replied. "Yeah, she one of the strippers here. You want me to get her over here? " Carlos asked. "Naw, I'm finna get her myself!" Vito said as he jumped from the couch and placed his Moet bottle on the table. Vito quickly made a beeline straight over to where she was and stood there for a few seconds as she and a few other women delivered the bottles. The moment they started to walk away from the group of men, Vito stepped in front of the woman he was interested in, she stood there and looked at him awkwardly trying to figure out why he blocked her path. "Excuse me, but I noticed you from across the room and I had to come over and get your name. So, what's your name?" Vito asked as he looked down at her. "My name is Cocoa" she replied with a smirk on her face. Cocoa was 18 years old, and fairly new in her stripping career, but was a beautiful bombshell. She stood there five feet tall, a mix of African American and Caucasian heritage, her Coke bottle shape was to die for, measuring 28 inches at the waist with 45-inch hips. Cocoa was the woman Vito always dreamt of having and there was no way he was leaving the club without being able to get in contact with her. "Cocoa, huh? I like that name. So, Cocoa, I know you working, so I ain't going to hold you up, but I wanna know is there any way I could get your number so I could get to know you outside of this setting?" Vito asked before licking his lips. Cocoa laughed a little. She found his approach a little corny, but she thought he was cute. She could tell by the diamond flooded Rolex on his wrist that he had some money so she figured she could profit somehow by fucking with him. "Yeah, you cute or whatever. I guess I wouldn't mind getting to know you!" Cocoa said before giving him her number then walking away.

Vito called Cocoa a few days later and was shocked when he discovered that she was really from Beloit, Wisconsin. He had talked Cocoa into going out on a date with him later that evening. On that first date, Cocoa took a major liking to Vito and wanted to continue seeing him, so that's just what she did. Vito and Cocoa made it official after two months of meeting each other. Vito felt like—now that Cocoa was his woman—she had to change her career, which was a win-win for her. Vito spoiled her with the latest cars, the finest jewelry, and filled her closet with the latest designer clothing. Vito decided it was best if he didn't shit in the same city, he laid his head, so he started spending most of his time in Beloit where he was not known.

Vito and Cocoa lived peacefully in Beloit as Vito continued to make drops and pickups from Milwaukee. Everything was going good, until one afternoon, Vito pulled to his stash house. He got out the car and walked up the steps and into the spot. Just as he began to pull money from his safe, the Feds kicked the door in. Vito was caught red-handed with six bricks of cocaine and two .9mm that Carlos had given him two months after he made it home. Vito quickly found out that Carlos had been working with the government and had become an informant for the Feds. Two years before Vito got out of prison, Carlos was caught on I-95 with two bricks of cocaine and immediately made a deal to work as an informant.

Vito later found out that one of the .9mm he got from Carlos had a body on it. Carlos told the Feds that he had information on a homicide and that he knew where the gun was being kept. Vito couldn't believe what was happening. He knew he hadn't murdered anyone, so he went to trial. Failing to realize that Carlos had already proved himself as a credible informant, Vito was found guilty on one count of first-degree intentional homicide, one count of possession with the intent to deliver a thousand or more grams of cocaine, along with felon in possession of a firearm. Snapping out of his trance, Vito walked out of his cell and headed to the phone to call Cocoa.

April 2019

Marguerite stood outside the gate of the Columbia Correctional Institution eagerly waiting for her first-born son Keef to be released. Every second seemed like hours as she smoked cigarette after cigarette. She tapped her feet up and down against the gravel as the wind blew harder and harder. "Marguerite, get in the car, girl! It's too cold out there" Denise said as she yelled from the inside of her truck. Marguerite looked back at Denise and blew out a cloud of smoke. When she turned back around, she noticed Keef walking to the gate and started jumping up and down as she yelled out "Oh my God! My baby out! My baby out!" Marguerite dropped her cigarette and took off running in his direction. Denise got out of the car. She had been waiting ten years for this moment to come and now Keef was finally free. Keef, now 29 years old, 6'3" and 225 pounds of straight muscle, with long dreads down to his chest. Keef smiled as he walked out the prison gates opening his arms wide to embrace his mother as if she were his child. Marguerite jumped into Keef's arms and hugged him. "God, thank you! Thank you!" she yelled as she kissed Keef on his cheeks. "It feels good to be out. I missed you!" Keef said to his mother. "Yes, you out now, baby. I missed you too!" Marguerite said as she cried. Keef started laughing. "Don't cry" he said as he held her. Denise stood off at a distance as she watched Keef and his mother hug one another. "Get over here and show me some love!" Keef said as he looked over at Denise. "Oh, I'm sorry!" Marguerite said as she broke away from their hug. Denise smiled as she walked over to Keef and gave him a huge hug. Keef placed his hand on the back of Denise's neck and started kissing her as he glided his other hand down to her lower back and cuffed her ass while he pulled her closer to him. "Damn, I missed you!" Keef said as he broke away from their kiss. "I missed you too, baby" Denise said as she gave him another peck on the lips. "Where dat nigga Keimon at?" Keef asked. "I don't know. He said he had something to do, but he'll stop by later" Marguerite said as she rushed back to the truck. "Yeah, let's hurry up and put this mafucka in my rearview" Keef said as he put his arm over Denise's shoulder and started walking towards the truck. Keimon turned onto Church Hill and parked his 2019 Mercedes Benz G-class 550 G wagon in front of Gabrielle's duplex. Gabrielle stood on the porch looking at Keimon as he jumped out of his truck. Keimon now 29 years old 6'3"and 215 pounds with a natural muscular build, with a bald fade and big beard, had come a long way since Keef went to prison in 2009. Keimon graduated from high school that year and went off to college at Marquette University on a four-year scholarship. He graduated with a Bachelor of Science in Business

Administration and went on to work for a major accounting firm in Atlanta. In 2015, Keimon parted ways with the firm and opened his own real estate company based in Atlanta as well.

"What's good?" Keimon said to Gabrielle as he got out of his truck. "I'm doing fine! I see you looking good as always!" Gabrielle said as she watched Keimon walk up to her front porch dripping in Givenchy from head to toe. "I try, I try!" Keimon said as he laughed and pulled Gabrielle close and gave her a hug. "So, what's going on? What was so important that you needed me to rush over here?" Keimon asked as he broke away from their hug. "It's Kutta!" Gabrielle responded. "What about him?" Keimon quickly asked. "He robbed Stacey after I made the drop last night." Gabrielle murmured, knowing Keimon was about to grow in a fit of rage. "What? Wait, why the hell am I just now hearing about this? How much did he take?" Keimon demanded to know. Gabrielle put her head down before looking Keimon directly into his eyes. "He took four bricks, I didn't call 'cause I wanted to see if we could get it back first" Gabrielle said. "Damn, Gab! You lucky I love you. Look, Imma handle it. Send a few of the guys over there with Stacey to make sure shit goes smooth from here on out" Keimon said as he put his hand on Gabrielle's shoulder. "I gotta get up out of here, the nigga Keef got out today. I gotta welcome bro home" Keimon quickly added before walking off. "I'm on it, ASAP!" Gabrielle responded before Keimon got out of earshot of her.

Kutta and his right-hand man, Dewight, sat in the living room at Kutta's crib on Red Arrow Trail. Dewight and Kutta clicked well because they were total opposites. Dewight is

6'4"and 250 pounds, the smooth, outspoken and friendly type. Kutta's 6'0" and 185 pounds. He's quiet, impetuous, and hated by many. Their common factors are their loyalty to each other and their love for the almighty dollar.

"Bro, I got some shit I wanna show you" Kutta said to Dewight before getting up and walking to the back room. He walked back into the living room and tossed a pillowcase on the coffee table. "Fuck is that?" Dewight asked as he sat up from the couch. "You remember last night when I was telling you about that stain? Well, I slid through that bitch anyway. I got four bricks up out that bitch!" Kutta said as he smiled and emptied the bag on the table. Dewight sat there shaking his head as he ran his hand over his beard. "Damn folks, you don't fuck around!" Dewight said as he picked a brick up off the table. "You went in there by yourself?" he asked before Kutta could say anything. "Hell yeah! I caught Stacey coming out the building and walked her ass back in the crib. She gave that shit up with no problem!" Kutta said as he chuckled. "You was masked up?" Dewight asked. "For what? That bitch ass nigga Keimon ain't gone do shit, bro, he don't want no smoke! Nigga, fuck all the questions and shit, you tryna get this money or not?" Kutta asked straight up.

Chapter Three

* * * * *

Kutta sat in the passenger seat rolling up a backwood as Dewight drove down Hammersley Road in his 2016 Chevy Malibu. It had been three days since Kutta took four bricks of cocaine from Stacey and sold them to Dewight's cousin. They wasted no time getting to work. Neither of the two had any interest in selling cocaine, but both had major clientele when it came to heroin.

"Pull over on Park Ridge and park. I'm finna pull up!" Dewight said before hanging up the phone. He reached over and picked up his cup of lean and took a sip from it. "This bitch rolling!" Dewight said as he placed his cup back in the holder. "It's been knocking all day!" Kutta quickly added as he lighted flame to the backwood. Kutta looked down when his phone began to rattle in the cup holder. "Yeah, this bitch jumping today!" Kutta said as he swiftly grabbed his phone then inhaled and exhaled a cloud of smoke. "What up?" he asked as he answered. *I'm passing Park Street, where you wanna meet?* the woman on the other end of the phone asked. "Call me when you hit Gammon!" Kutta ordered. *Alright,* the woman said before hanging up.

Kutta dropped his phone back into his lap as he took another hit from his backwood. "Bro, you not going to believe who I fucked last night!" Kutta said as he exhaled a cloud of smoke and passed the backwood over to Dewight. "Who?" Dewight asked as he made a right turn on to Gammon. "Jessie!" Kutta said as he smiled ear to ear. Dewight made a right turn on the next street before looking over at Kutta. "You talking about red bone Jessie?" Dewight asked as he made a right turn onto Park Ridge. "Hell yeah!" Kutta said with honor as he grabbed the backwood back and took a hit from it. Dewight picked up his phone and dialed his people's number. "Follow me!" Dewight ordered as he drove past them. "Did she have some good pussy?" Dewight asked as he put his phone back into his lap. Kutta laughed and looked over at Dewight "My nigga, she a boss freak! That's all Imma say!" Kutta replied "Imma have to put her on my list!" Dewight said as he pulled over and put the car into park. "On BD!" Kutta responded as he watched the small frail white woman jump from the passenger side of the car behind them from his side mirror. Dewight unlocked the car doors as the woman got closer to the car. She opened the car door and jumped into the back seat and closed the door. She tossed a fistful of balled up twenty-dollar bills on Dewight's lap. "What's this?" Dewight asked. "It's eight hundred. I need four!" she responded. "Ight!" he said before he reached back and handed her four grams. The woman jumped out of the car as quickly as she had gotten in and rushed back to her car. "Where yo people at? Dewight asked Kutta as he pulled off.

Meanwhile

Keimon and Keef pulled in front of the Impala Hotel on Collins Avenue in Miami Beach, Florida and parked. Keimon had set up a meeting with the Funcesca brothers in hopes of bringing his brother into their inner circle. The Funcescas are a sophisticated group of Dominican brothers with major connections throughout the Dominican Republic, South America, and the US. The Funcescas supply Keimon with some of the purest cocaine out of Colombia. "Look, bro, these niggas don't play no games. They weird in their own way and they got mad reach, so let me do the talking" Keimon said as he looked over at Keef. "I got you, bro!" Keef said as he nervously sat in the passenger seat. He had never been this deep in the drug game, so this was unfamiliar territory for him.

Keimon jumped out of his 2019 Aston Martin DBS Superleggera Volante wearing a tailor-made white linen Yves Saint Laurent suit, with a pair of red Yves Saint Laurent loafers. His Bustdown Audemar watch and his custom-made Graduated Baguette necklace complemented his attire. Keef got out of the passenger side wearing a royal blue Givenchy button down shirt, all white Givenchy linen pants, and a pair of royal blue Louis Junior spiked Louis Orlato flats. His gold iced out Cartier glasses matched his custom Icebox Rolex. Keef followed Keimon into the hotel entrance and over to its restaurant. Keimon scanned the room looking for the Funcesca brothers. He spotted the brothers in the back looking like three corporate white men and made his way over to their table. As Keimon and Keef approached the table the brothers stood up and greeted Keimon by shaking his hand. "I want to introduce you all to my twin brother, Keef. Keef, this is Carlos, Waun, and Pito" Keimon quickly said. "Nice to meet you!" Keef said as he shook their hands. "Have a seat" Pito said as he pointed to the two empty chairs at the table. They all sat down. "Keef, it's nice to meet you. We've heard a lot about you. Your brother really admires you, which he should, 'cause we believe family loyalty is most important" Carlos said before taking a sip from his glass of water. "It's nice to meet you as well. I also believe in family loyalty cause without family there's nothing." Keef said as he gave a nervous smile. The group of men sat silent for a moment, which made Keef increasingly uneasy. "Let me be frank with you, Keef. Normally, we would never invite your kind in, but your brother has shown us that he's an honorable man, and insured us that loyalty runs in his blood. So, because of that, I'm going to officially invite you in on Keimon's name alone" Waun said in a thick Dominican accent. "Trust me, you won't regret your decision" Keef replied. "Great!" Waun responded before looking to Keimon. "I acquired the deed to the thirty acres of land in Virginia you inquired about at our last sit down. Add another six hundred thousand on top of the two hundred million for the last shipment and we'll be squared away" Waun added. "I appreciate you making that happen for me. I been trying to buy that land for over a year and a half now. If you don't mind me asking, how did you get him to sell?" Keimon asked. "Sometimes you have to apply a little pressure, that with the right incentives!" Waun said as he and his brother chuckled on their inside joke. Keimon felt his phone vibrate in his pocket as he laughed a little at what Waun just said. "Fellas, excuse me a moment!" Keimon said after he pulled his phone from his pocket and recognized it was Gabrielle's number. "What up?" Keimon quickly asked as he got up and walked away from the table. *He said he wants twenty thousand!* Gabrielle responded. "Look, I don't care what he wants, make sure it gets done. Make sure your hands stay clean, we don't need this shit to be traced back to us!" Keimon ordered as he whispered. *Okay, I got you*, Gabrielle said before ending the call. Keimon stood there for a moment thinking, he knew Kutta was a problem and he needed to be dealt with, or else everyone would be trying to get at him. He couldn't allow that to happen. Keimon turned and walked back over to the table and finished handling business.

Meanwhile

Three days had passed since the robbery and Cocoa still hadn't returned home. Afraid that someone would return to her home, she decided to stay with her mom for a while. Determined not to let the setback keep her down, she put things in overdrive. As long as she had her phones, she knew she could make the money back. Cocoa had a new recruit on her team named Marsai. Marsai is a 25-year-old natural Puerto Rican beauty standing at 5'3" and 130 pounds. Her petite body frame complemented her perfect ass and perky breasts. For the past two days, Cocoa had been getting nonstop calls from Johns that wanted Marsai over her other girls.

Marsai pulled into the driveway of a two-story house in Rockford, Illinois and parked her Chevy truck. She flipped down her sun visor and looked in her mirror to check her make-up. She picked up her phone looking at the time.

Realizing it was 11:00 pm, she quickly dialed Cocoa's number. *Hello*, Cocoa said as she answered the phone. "It's me, Marsai, I'm calling to let you know I made it. I'm about to go in now." Marsai said. *Okay, call me if you need anything*, Cocoa responded. "Okay" Marsai said before she ended the call. Marsai fixed her hair, then put her phone back in her purse before jumping out of her truck, wearing an ash grey off the shoulder Prada dress with black heels. She walked up to the front door and rang the doorbell. A short, chubby Mexican man in his late thirties opened the door. He stood there for a moment looking at Marsai as if she were a steak and he hadn't eaten in weeks. "Hi, I take it you're Alex" Marsai said bringing Alex back to reality. "Yeah, I'm Alex, I take it you're Marsai" Alex replied. "Yup!" Marsai said. "Come on in" Alex said as he opened the door further allowing Marsai to enter. Marsai walked in and stood steps inside the doorway. Alex closed the door and locked it. "Before I go any further it'll be two thousand five hundred dollars. Five hundred an hour." Marsai said as Alex turned to face her. "I see you're a straight shooter" Alex said as he reached into his pocket and pulled out a fistful of cash. Alex quickly counted off the money and handed it to Marsai. "Follow me" Alex said as he walked past Marsai and turned into the living room. Marsai tucked the money into her purse and followed Alex into the living room.

Meanwhile

Dewight pulled in front of Jessie's crib on Turbot and parked. He reached over to the passenger seat and shook Kutta and woke him up. "Aye, folks, we at shorty crib!" Kutta looked at him trying to figure out what was going on. "Damn, folks on BD, that drank crept up on me. Let's slide in here for a minute and see what they on in here" Kutta said as he adjusted his 9mm on his waist, opened the door and jumped out. Dewight took the keys from the ignition and jumped out of the car and followed Kutta up to Jessie's building.

Kutta pulled his keys from his pocket and unlocked the building door. "Damn folks, you got keys already!" Dewight said as he laughed. "You know, I don't fuck around!" Kutta responded. "What y'all in a relationship or something?" Dewight asked. Kutta laughed a little and looked back at Dewight. "Naw, that's just my friend I just got some keys so I can slide through when I need to" Kutta said then lead the way upstairs to Jessie's apartment. As he unlocked the door, he could smell the aroma of fried chicken. "On BD, that shit smell good as a bitch!" Kutta said as Dewight closed and locked the door. Jessie 5'7and, 150 pounds red bone is what some would call slim, came walking from the back room when she heard Kutta's voice. "Hey, Dewight!" Jessie said as she walked into the kitchen. "What up!" Dewight responded as he took a seat on the living room sofa. Kutta made his way into the kitchen. "What you cook with that chicken?" Kutta asked as Jessie looked through the fridge. "Just some macaroni, corn, and biscuits. You want a plate right now?" Jessie asked. "Hell yeah!" Kutta said as he took a seat at the kitchen table and pulled an ounce of weed from his pocket and placed it on it. "What about you, Dewight, do you want a plate?" Jessie said loud enough for Dewight to hear. "Hell yeah!" Dewight said as he flipped through his phone. "Where your buddy at?" Kutta asked Jessie as he began to break down a cigarillo. "She in the back watching TV. Why you ask?" Jessie asked. "'Cause I wanna see if she got an ass like yours!" Kutta responded. "Boy, you too thirsty!" Jessie quickly shot back. "Damn, why I gotta be thirsty? I call it curious!" Kutta said as he began to break the weed down into the blunt. "Yeah, okay! She in the back. Go back there and kill your curiosity. So, do you want me to make this plate before or after you smoke that?" Jessie asked. "You can make the plates now, Imma smoke this when I'm done!" Kutta said before he stood up and made his way to Jessie's room.

He walked into the room and found a short, dark-skinned female laying across Jessie's bed, as he walked further into the room to get a good look at her, he noticed she was thick as hell. "Damn… what's your name?" Kutta asked. She glanced over at him before looking back to the TV. "My name is Kim" she responded. "I'm Kutta, it's nice to meet you, Kim!" Kutta said as he stood there rolling his blunt. "Nice to meet you too, Kutta" Kim said while never looking away from the TV. "Alright, now that we got that out the way, I gotta say you thick as hell, Kim" Kutta said as he licked his blunt closed. Kim's eyes shot from the TV over to Kutta as she laughed from shock at his boldness. "I know that already!" Kim said in a sassy tone. "I know you know, but I wanna let you know that I noticed it as well!" Kutta replied. Kim laughed a little. "Kutta, leave my damn friend alone! Your food in there on the table" Jessie said as she walked into the room. "That's crazy, I was just getting to know Kim. I was just about to ask her what's her favorite color and all that shit!" Kutta said then started laughing. Kim and Jessie both started laughing. "Kutta get yo ass out my room!" Jessie said as she laughed and pushed Kutta out the room.

Chapter Four

* * * * *

While Dewight was laid up in the hospital, Kutta stood in E.A.'s living room loading up his Smith & Wesson SD40 pistol. He didn't know the identity of the shooter, but he didn't have to second guess where the hit came from. "That bitch ass nigga Keimon gotta die! He sent that nigga my way and now he finna regret not killing me." Kutta said as he began to pace back and forth through the living room. "So, what's the plan'?" E.A. asked while sitting on the sofa. "I don't know. But what I do know for sure is that he fucked with Stacey. I wanna slide on her and see what she know" Kutta replied. "You talking about Stacey on Rimrock?" E.A. quickly asked with a curious look on his face. "Yeah! Why you say it like that?" Kutta asked. "'Cause I know Stacey lil brothers. They be itching to slide on some shit, it might have been one of them niggas" E.A. responded. "Bro, if they fuck with Stacey, or that nigga Keimon, they going to get it anyway 'cause somebody finna pay the price for what they did to folks" Kutta said. "Shit, we can slide on them niggas tonight; I know where they be at!" E.A. said as he rubbed his hands together. "Yeah, we on they ass then! But let's jump in traffic real quick, I gotta get this money. I ain't got no time to waste." Kutta said as he tucked his .40 in his pants.

Meanwhile

Keef pulled up to LAX to pick up Scooter. Scooter had been released from prison earlier that morning, so Keimon put him on the first flight to LA. Keef wanted to welcome him home the right way. He hadn't seen Scooter since they both got kicked out of Green Bay Correctional in 2013 for battery to an inmate. Keef pulled up to the air terminal in a 2020 Range Rover LWB V8 Supercharged. He instantly put the car into park and jumped out when he noticed Scooter standing there looking around. "Scooter!" Keef yelled out as he rushed over to him. "Man, my nigga, it's good to see you!" Scooter said as he smiled and shook Keef's hand. "Man, I know it's been a while, but we out here now. Let's go turn up my nigga, it's our turn now" Keef responded. "I see you driving that Range Rover! Shit, I ain't never been in a Range before!" Scooter said as he looked at the china blue Range Rover. "That ain't shit, bro! Here, you can drive!" Keef said as he tossed the keys to Scooter.

Scooter rushed over to the truck and jumped in. Keef jumped into the passenger seat and closed the door. Scooter put the car into drive and headed out of LAX. "Where the hell am I driving to?" Scooter asked. "Make a left, then make a left two lights up, we going to North Hollywood. Keimon got a mansion over there we firma party like you ain't never partied before!" Keef said as he turned the music up and Lil Baby's song "Humble" poured from the speakers.

After a twenty-minute drive, Scooter made a right turn as directed by Keef into a driveway and parked in front of the gate. Keef jumped out of the truck and put the code in then stood there as the gate opened. In a waving motion, he directed Scooter to drive forward. Scooter pulled through the gate and stopped as he waited for Keef to get back into the truck. As they drove up the driveway, Scooter couldn't believe how large they were living. When he left, Keimon wasn't on shit, and they were all sharing each other's clothes. Now, Keimon was living large having things he could only dream of owning. Keimon had also took care of Scooter his entire bid making sure he wanted for nothing. He figured Keimon was doing okay, but not to this extent. Scooter pulled in front of the brick mansion and was mesmerized at all of the different exotic cars parked in the huge driveway.

"Damn, niggas driving Rolls-Royces! I'm loving this shit already!" Scooter quickly said as he smiled. Keef jumped out the truck and walked up the stairs to the front porch and opened the huge sixteen-foot wooden doors and walked into the huge foyer. Scooter was mind-blown when he walked in behind Keef, the marble flooring and high ceilings were something to marvel at. "This bitch look like a castle, my nigga!" Scooter said shocked as he looked around. "That nigga Keimon own this shit?" Scooter asked in disbelief. Keef laughed a little as he walked further into the mansion and through the rotunda. He walked over to a door on the left side of the rotunda, opened it, and made his way downstairs to the rumpus room. The rumpus room was a room like no other. It was humongous and resembled a night club; it had everything that a young bachelor could want. A stage with three stripper poles was strategically placed in the center of the room. A huge bar wrapped along the left side of the room with every kind of liqueurs and liquors, from absinthe to triple sec, bourbon to vodka. Along the right side, there were many pool tables and many other games from darts to foosball. There was also a large seating area with many red button-back sofas and a large 120-inch flat screen mounted on the wall.

"WELCOME HOME!" everyone in the packed room yelled as Scooter entered the room. He was shocked and caught completely off-guard. He scanned the crowd of unfamiliar faces and recognized Keimon. "Welcome home, bro!" Keimon said as he approached Scooter. "Damn, I ain't seen you in a long ass time. I see you doing real good for yourself. I'm loving this shit, bro!" Scooter said as he scanned the room. "Yeah, I know. The last time I seen you was when you got sentenced. My bad on not coming to see you. I ain't wanna see y'all niggas locked up in a cage" Keimon quickly responded. "It's all love!" Scooter quickly replied. Keimon turned and looked over to the seating area and waved Alesha over to him. "Aye, bro, I got something for you! But first, Alesha finna get that monkey off your back. It look like it's heavy too, bro!" Keimon said as he laughed. "What's going on?" Alesha asked as she walked up to Scooter and Keimon. " Aye, Alesha, this my brother Scooter. I want to you take him upstairs and take care of him. It's been ten years, so take it easy on him." Keimon said then reached down and slapped Alesha on the ass. "Anything for you, daddy!" Alesha said to Keimon as she grabbed a hold of Scooter's hand and led him back up the stairs.

Alesha took Scooter to the first guest bedroom down the hall from the kitchen and closed the door. She walked him over to the bed and began kissing him on the neck. "I ain't on all of that!" Scooter said as he stopped her. "Okay, so what do you want?" Alesha asked. "You got some condoms?" Scooter asked her. "Yes" Alesha said as she reached over to the nightstand and pulled out some condoms. "Ight, cool" Scooter said then grabbed the condom, opened it savagely, and pulled down his pants to put it on. He turned Alesha around and bent her over the bed, pulling her panties to the side and forcefully began to thrust inside of her. Alesha let out a soft moan, shocked at his aggressiveness. Scooter began to pound her harder and harder with each thrust. It didn't take Scooter two minutes before he exploded. He pulled out, took the condom off, and slapped Alesha on her ass. He then walked out of the room. He wanted to treat her just like the ho' she was.

Meanwhile

Ricky sat in the back of Kutta's Jeep Grand Cherokee trying to persuade Kutta into letting him hold another gram after he hadn't paid the five hundred dollars, he already owed. E.A. began to grow impatient as Ricky continued to beg. "Look, Ricky, you ain't got shit coming! Once you pay folks the bread you owe, then he gone look out for you. In the meantime, you gotta get yo ass out, we got shit to do!" E.A. said as he turned in the passenger seat to face Ricky in the back seat. "Kutta, come on, man. I need you! I promise if you get me right, Imma take care of you. You know I'm good for it. I spend plenty of money with you" Ricky begged as he itched his neck and arms. "Damn, Ricky. Man, I ain't finna play with you, if you don't come with my bread, you can lose my number!" Kutta said as he reached back and handed Ricky a gram. Kutta hated having his people out there bad, 'cause he knew they needed it to survive. Plus, he figured if they were ever to get in a jam, he would be the last one they give up 'cause he always made sure they got what they needed. "Thank you, Kutta. I promise Imma take care of you" Ricky said as he jumped out the back of the Jeep and rushed back to his car.

"On BD, bro, that's Stacey lil brothers right there!" E.A. shouted to Kutta as he pointed to a green Monte Carlo with tinted windows that pulled over and parked about five cars ahead of them. "On BD, I'm on they ass! You sure that's them?" Kutta asked. "Dave, that's them!" E.A. replied. "Alright, pull my car around the corner. I'm finna get they ass!" Kutta said as he pulled his hoodie from the back seat and pulled it over his head then jumped out of the jeep. E.A. speedily jumped over into the driver seat and threw the car into drive and made a U-turn in the opposite direction. Kutta stood next to a tree as he waited for E.A. to turn the corner. Just as E.A. turned the corner, Kutta pulled the hood over his head and pulled his .40 from his waist and tucked it into his hoodie pocket then ducked down on the side of a car. He crept past three cars, then walked in between two cars so that he could get on the driver side. He wanted to make sure they couldn't pull off. Just as Kutta began to creep through the street, a female came out a house from across the street and started walking up to the Monte Carlo, completely overlooking him. He had a very big decision to make. In a matter of seconds, it was either let them get away, or get her too. The driver's door opened up to allow her to get into the back seat. She looked up and noticed him on the approach and froze in her tracks.

Kutta popped up to the driver's door and shot her once in the chest, then popped three shots into the back of the driver's head, splattering his brains all over the dashboard. The passenger jumped out the car and took off running up the street. Kutta started chasing after him. He let off two shots hitting him once in the leg, causing him to fall. "Please, please!" he begged as he laid on his back with his arms covering his face. "Fuck you, bitch ass nigga!" Kutta said as he ran up on him and shot him three more times, killing him. Kutta took off running in between two houses.

Meanwhile

It was 7:00 pm in California and Scooter had just finished getting dressed. He made his way back downstairs to the rumpus room to enjoy his welcome home party. "There my nigga go! It took you long enough to get back to the party!" Keef yelled over from the bar area. "Man, bro, I needed that. I had to wash the prison from my body, now I'm back! They done fucked up by letting me out!" Scooter said. "What you wanna drink?" Keimon asked. "I don't know, something strong!" Scooter replied as he looked around the room. "Give my man a double shot of Hennessy!" Keimon ordered. "Who the fuck is all these people?" Scooter asked. "These my people!" Keimon said. "I know you remember Gabrielle and Stacey. We went to school with them!" Keimon added as he pointed over to them across the room. "Gabrielle over there?

You know I was on her line before I got locked up!" Scooter said then quickly slammed the double shot he was handed. "Let me get another one!" Scooter said as he looked at the woman behind the bar. "Bro, you might wanna take it easy, you know you a lightweight. You been gone too long to be killing drinks like that!" Keef chimed in. "Yeah, that's Gab!" Keimon said before Scooter could respond to Keef. "Bro, it's my welcome home party. I'm about to get drunk, then fuck the shit out of one of these bitches, preferably Gabrielle" Scooter said. Keef and Keimon both looked at each other. Neither wanted to tell Scooter that Keimon had been fucking Gabrielle. The bartender handed Scooter another double shot of Hennessy. Scooter downed it, then slammed the glass on the bar. "Ooooh, shit!" Scooter huffed as the Hennessy burned his chest, then he looked over at Keimon. "So, you built all this off that bread we got from that Arabian nigga crib?" Scooter asked. Keimon and Keef looked at each other as they both caught the vibe Scooter was giving off. "Naw, my nigga! I built all this off my cut of what we got out that crib. I took care of y'all and y'all lawyer fees with the rest" Keimon said. "Aye, let's see what's to these hoes" Keef said as he pulled Scooter from the bar without giving him a chance to respond.

He knew Scooter was used to always being the one making a way for them to be able to come up, and Keimon being the one following them. But those days were no more, it was a new day, and before he would allow Scooter to fuck the night up, he moved him around. Keimon stayed at the bar thinking, his gut feeling was telling him that Scooter might become a problem. He didn't like the feeling because he considered Scooter a brother, but he knew he had to follow that feeling and keep his eyes open.

Back in Beloit

Marsai had just pulled into town. After her crazy night at Alex's house, she drove straight to her parents' house in Racine. Marsai was still shook up and didn't even wanna go outside, but she had to meet up with Cocoa. Marsai pulled her phone from her purse as she drove down Prairie and dialed Cocoa's number and waited for her to answer. *Hey, Marsai* Cocoa said as she answered the phone. "Hey girl, where you at?" Marsai asked. *I'm on Dewey. Where you at?* Cocoa asked. "I'm about to turn on Henry right now" Marsai replied. *Okay, well pull up and park behind my car I'm sitting out on the porch*, Cocoa said. "Okay" Marsai replied, then ended the call.

Marsai turned onto Henry, then drove a few blocks up and made a left turn on Dewey. As she made her way up the block, she noticed Cocoa's Lexus and parked behind it. She reached into the back seat and grabbed the duffle bag and put it on the passenger seat. She was so frightened after what happened at Alex's house, she never looked back in the bag.

Cocoa walked up to Marsai's truck and opened the door. "How you feeling, girl?" Cocoa asked. "I'm still shook up from that shit" Marsai replied as she ran her hands through her hair. "Girl, I been getting nonstop calls for you. What you been doing to them niggas?" Cocoa asked as she laughed a little trying to lighten the mood. "Nothing, really, girl. I guess I got that good good!" Marsai said as laughed a little. "Yeah, you must have it cause they loving them some you. I just been telling them you're out of town. You don't have to rush back" Cocoa said. "Okay, 'cause that shit scared the hell out of me. I think when I go back, I'm going to need some security" Marsai said. "So, this is what I found" Marsai added as she pointed to the duffle bag. Cocoa reached into the truck and unzipped the duffle bag. "Oh shit!" Cocoa said as she noticed the four bricks of heroin and a stack of cash inside the bag. She jumped into the truck and closed the door. "What's wrong?" Marsai asked. "Nothing at all!" Cocoa said. She knew that Marsai didn't know much about drugs and that she would do whatever she said, plus she needed to take full advantage of this. She grabbed the stack of cash and fanned through it. "This looks like about twenty thousand. Here, take this, it should hold you over until you're ready to get back to work" Cocoa said as she handed the stack of cash to Marsai. "You sure?" Marsai asked. "Yeah, girl, you gotta live and I wanna make sure you're straight" Cocoa said. "Thanks, girl!" Marsai replied. "It ain't no problem. Now I need to go put this up. What you about to do?" Cocoa asked Marsai as she zipped the duffle bag up. "I'm about to go home and rest" Marsai replied. "Okay, I'm going to stop by after I take care of this. I got a bottle of Patron if you want to have a few drinks" Cocoa said. "Yeah, that's fine, just call me" Marsai replied. "Alright, I will" Cocoa said as she opened the truck door then jumped out. "See you later!" Marsai said as Cocoa closed the door. Cocoa hurried and walked over to her car and popped the trunk, tossed the duffle bag in, and closed it. She was happy that this just fell into her lap so easily. She knew if she just sold the four bricks wholesale, she was going to make three hundred sixty thousand dollars.

Cocoa pulled her phone from her pocket, jumped into her Lexus, and pulled off.

Meanwhile

It was now 9:15pm in California and Scooter was drunk and really enjoying himself. After enjoying a few drinks and meeting some of Keimon's people, he looked up and seen Stacey and Gabrielle dancing with each other over by the seating area. Scooter had been liking Gabrielle since eighth grade and figured now was his chance to get her. He made his way over to where Stacey and Gabrielle were dancing and tapped Gabrielle on her shoulder. Stacey's phone started to ring, so she answered it and walked off. Gabrielle turned around and smiled when she seen Scooter. "Hey, Scooter" Gabrielle said as she looked at him. "It's been a long time since I last seen you. How you been?" Scooter asked. "I've actually been doing good. It has been a long time... I haven't seen you since the twelfth grade. I know you're happy to be out. So, tell me, how are you enjoying the party?" Gabrielle asked. "I'm happy to be a free man. I got the chance to get my life back on track, so that's what I'm planning to do. I'm enjoying the party, but most of these people I don't even know, but I can say it's good to see familiar faces like yours" Scooter said as he smiled.

Gabrielle glanced over at Stacey and immediately noticed something was wrong from the look on her face. "It's good to see you too, Scooter. I don't mean to be rude, but I need to check on my friend" Gabrielle said when she noticed Stacey had started crying. Gabrielle walked off and over to where Stacey stood talking on the phone. "What's wrong?" Gabrielle asked Stacey. Stacey looked up at Gabrielle and started crying even harder. "What's wrong?" Gabrielle asked again. "They killed my brothers!" Stacey said as she hung the phone up. Gabrielle pulled Stacey close to her and gave her a hug. "I'm so sorry!" Gabrielle said as she held Stacey. "I can't believe my brothers are dead. I gotta go home!" Stacey said as she broke away from Gabrielle and walked away. Gabrielle looked around for Keimon before she spotted him at the bar talking to Keef. Scooter stood off to the side as he watched Gabrielle make a beeline straight to Keimon. "I really need to talk to you, it's important" Gabrielle said as she approached Keimon. "What's wrong?" Keimon asked seeing the panic in Gabrielle's eyes. "We need to go upstairs" Gabrielle said then walked off towards the stairs. "I'll be right back, bro" Keimon said to Keef before he jumped up from his stool and followed Gabrielle upstairs. Scooter stood and watched Gabrielle and Keimon walk up the stairs before he walked over to the bar with Keef.

Gabrielle walked into the kitchen and looked around to see if anyone was around before she started talking. "So, what's up, Gab?" Keimon asked. "We got a problem! Something went wrong, the two niggas I hired to do the hit got killed today. But the worst thing is that they're Stacey's little brothers!" Gabrielle said as her eyes filled with tears. "What the fuck, Gab?! I told you to make sure this shit don't blow back on us, and you go and hire her brothers!" Keimon was pissed. "I know I fucked up! But we gotta do something about this fast!" Gabrielle said as she began to panic. Gabrielle knew that this shit could land on her doorstep just as fast as it found Stacey's brothers and she didn't want that to happen. "Look, do Stacey know 'bout this?" Keimon asked. "Yeah, she the one who told me" Gabrielle said. "Damn! Look, don't worry, I'm about to handle this. I gotta put y'all on the first flight back to Madison. I need to know what's the word on the street" Keimon said. "Alright, I'm about to go get Stacey and make sure she's alright" Gabrielle said. "Yeah, go do that!" Keimon said.

Gabrielle headed back down to the rumpus room. Keimon stood there for a moment, knowing Kutta knew by now that he sent the hit, he needed to hurry up and get him out of the way. Keimon pulled his phone from his pocket and dialed his cousin Von's number. *What up, skud?* Von asked as he answered the phone. "Shit cuz! Check it out, I keep having a problem with this roof, so I need a few of yo lil homies to come help me nail this roof down the right way. You got me?" Keimon asked. *It's official, skud. I got you. I'm firma line that up for you.* Von replied. "Ight, bet! I'm in Cali right now. I'll be back that way in two days." Keimon said. *Say no more, skud, it's done!* Von said. "Good looking!" Keimon replied. *Yup!* Von said, then ended the call.

Keimon put his phone back in his pocket, walked out of the kitchen, and headed back down to the rumpus room. Scooter and Keef sat at the bar drinking when Scooter looked up and seen Keimon walking back into the room. He watched as Keimon walked over to the seating area where Stacey and Gabrielle were sitting. Keimon walked over to them and put his hand on Stacey's shoulder. "I'm sorry about your brothers. I'll take care of the funeral arrangements, and if there is anything else you need, let me know" Keimon said as Stacey cried. "Aye, it's a 11:39 flight out of Cali back to

Chicago. I booked it for y'all. Imma need you to take Stacey home and take care of her" Keimon said to Gabrielle. "Okay, I got her" Gabrielle said. Stacey stood up and gave Keimon a hug. "If you want to do something for me, get the nigga that did this to my brothers" Stacey whispered into his ear. "On my life, I got you!" Keimon assured her. Stacey broke away from their hug and made her way over to the stairs. Scooter watched as Gabrielle gave Keimon a hug and a kiss, making his blood boil. Over the years, Scooter developed a hater's mentality from the caliber of niggas he was hanging with in prison. He was already jealous that Keimon had all the money now, but mix the liquor with his jealousy, and he was at his breaking point. Keimon had the girl he's had a crush on since eighth grade.

"Aye, give a double shot of Patron. Naw, matter of a fact, just give me the whole bottle" Keimon said as he walked up to the bar. "Damn, bro, you straight?" Keef asked. But before Keimon could respond, Scooter leaned over and chimed in. "Damn, bro, what you on some hating shit?" Scooter asked Keimon. Keimon looked up, shocked and confused as to what Scooter was talking about. "What? What the fuck you talking about, bro?" Keimon asked. "I told you earlier that I was trying to get Gabrielle, then I look up and you all hugged up kissing on her and shit" Scooter said. "Bro, you tripping, you drunk right now!" Keimon said. "But if you wanna know, I been fucking Gabrielle long before you got out!" Keimon added. "You know what I see what it is. You think you the shit 'cause you got some money, but remember, I know you. I know you a bitch!" Scooter yelled. "Bro, you trippin!" Keef also yelled as he stood up in between Keimon and Scooter. "You know what, Imma let you have that cause you drunk!" Keimon said. "You gone let me have it 'cause you a BITCH!" Scooter shouted across Keef at Keimon. Keimon got pissed off when Scooter's spit flew and landed on his face. "Watch out, bro!" Keimon said as he pushed Keef to the side and hit Scooter with a left hook, then a right one, dropping Scooter to the floor. "Now, show me I'm a bitch!" Keimon said as he got on top of Scooter and punched him a few more times. "Man, y'all niggas trippin!" Keef said as he pulled Keimon off of Scooter. "Now get this bitch ass nigga out my house!" Keimon ordered Keef before he walked off. "Now, EVERYBODY, get the fuck out! This shit over!" Keimon shouted then made his way up the stairs.

Chapter Five

* * * * *

Three days later

Dewight stood in the lobby of St. Mary's hospital waiting on his big cousin Tick to pick him up. Dewight pulled his phone from his pocket and just as he was about to dial Tick's number, he seen Tick's all white 840i BMW pull up. Dewight stood up and grabbed his crutches and hobbled out of the building. He hobbled over to the passenger side of the car, put his crutches in the back seat, then jumped into the passenger seat. Tick liked to be low-key, so he only fucked with the niggas that was really getting money. "What up, cuz?" Dewight asked as he closed the door and Tick pulled off. "Shit, cuz, you know me, staying out the way, but keeping my ears to these streets" Tick responded. "So, what the street talking 'bout?" Dewight asked. "You know I been fucking the lil bitch Stacey for a while now. So, I know that coke I bought from y'all came from them. The word is that the nigga Keimon put some bread on Kutta's head. Stacey's lil brothers got killed and now the streets whispering Kutta's name" Tick replied. "Damn, I seen that shit on the news, but I ain't know them was Stacey's brothers" Dewight said. "Well, look cuz, Imma keep it real with you, you might wanna keep yo distance from that nigga Kutta, 'cause I think them niggas firma try and get some get back after what happened to Stacey's lil brothers" Tick said.

Dewight looked over at him. He knew Tick was right, but Kutta was his brother and it wasn't no way he wasn't going to ride with him. "I know you just looking out for my best interest, cuz, and I respect that, but that's my man's. I'm riding with him til the wheels fall off. Just do me a favor and keep me posted on what Stacey over there talking about" Dewight asked. "You know I got you! It's a good thing mafuckas don't know we cousins, 'cause they more than willing to talk to me about it. Just do me a favor, cuz, and make sure you stay safe out here" Tick asked. "I got you, cuz!" Dewight said before he turned the music up and sat back.

Meanwhile

Keimon was sitting in the back of a Mercedes Benz Sprinter with T-mac, Red, and two other young niggas that came up from Chicago. The driver of the Sprinter pulled over and parked in front of one of Keimon's apartment buildings in Sun Prairie. "Come back and get me in thirty minutes" Keimon said to the driver as he opened the door and jumped out.

All four young niggas jumped out of the Sprinter and followed him into the building. Keimon walked into an empty apartment on the second floor, closed, and locked the door after everyone walked in. "Aye, check it out" Keimon said as he walked to the back room. They all followed Keimon into the back room, Keimon pulled a wooden crate from the closet and opened it up. "These American FN-15 pistols with a thirty-round capacity!" Keimon said as he pulled one from the crate and handed it to T-mac. T-mac is a dark-skinned 5'3"and 160-pound 20-year-old with a short man's complex. He's the oldest and the craziest of the four. T-mac was down to kill whoever, wherever, whenever without a second thought if the price was right. "So, what's the ticket on this mission?" T-mac asked. "I got ten thousand for each one of y'all up front and sixty thousand for the one that put a bullet in his face. I want his casket closed!" Keimon said. "Ight, I'm wit that!" T-mac said as he looked over at his cousin Red. Keimon pulled out another American FN-15 and handed it to Red. Red is also dark-skinned but he's a 6'2"and 190 pound 18-year-old. Red loved to be in competition with T-mac to see who can score the most and do a nigga the dirtiest. "I got two Tahoe trucks parked in the back. T-mac, I want you to take one, and Red you take the other one. Y'all can ride two deep that way y'all can stay low-key. Put one FN-15 in each truck and I got four SD9s in that crate, one for each of y'all" Keimon said. Keimon reached on to the top shelf in the closet and pulled down a black bag and reached in and grabbed the truck keys. He tossed one set to Red and the other to T-mac. He pulled out a stack of cash wrapped in rubber bands and handed each one ten thousand each. "Take these burner phones to keep in contact with each other. The nigga name Kutta, he drive a black Jeep Grand Cherokee. This what he look like!" Keimon said as he handed T-mac his phone. "Alright, I got it! I'm about to send this picture to the guys so we got it on deck" T-mac said before he sent the picture to his phone. "Here go the keys to the apartment next door, that's where y'all can stay until this shit is done. Keimon said giving T-mac the keys. "Ight" Red said as he looked over at Keimon. Red and T-mac had already become familiar with Madison a few years back when they came down to put some work in with Von Dutch, so they both knew the drill and the streets well.

Meanwhile
The next day

It was 9:15 am when Kutta pulled into Dewight's apartment complex on Tucson Trail. He parked his rental car and jumped out. He hadn't seen Dewight since the night he got shot and wanted to see what the police asked him. He walked up to the building and hit Dewight's buzzer. "Who is?" Dewight asked. "It's me, nigga!" Kutta replied. "Who the fuck is me?" Dewight joked. "Man, open the door!" Kutta responded. Dewight started laughing before he buzzed the door open. Kutta walked into the building, up the stairs to the apartment and opened the door. "Nigga, say yo name next time you ring my bell!" Dewight said as Kutta walked in. "Man, I ain't tryna hear that shit!" Kutta said as he closed and locked the door. "I see yo weak ass up and moving!" Kutta said as he laughed. "Nigga, that shit ain't funny! Yo weak ass got me hit up!" Dewight said as he hobbled over to the couch and sat down. "Now yo big ass got yo self-hit up. You know when them bullets get to flying, you gotta make yo self as little as possible." Kutta said before he pulled a 9mm from his waist and put it on the coffee table then sat down. "But fuck that shit, what's the word? What the law saying?"

Kutta asked. "Shit, my nigga, I told they ass I walked out of a bitch crib and niggas started shooting. I ended up getting hit and had shorty drive me to the hospital. You know they wasn't trying to hear that shit, but they ain't have no other choice" Dewight said. "Ight, that's what's up. But you know, you my nigga, so I wasn't gone let that shit go unanswered. I slid on them niggas like I was headed to second base. I rocked both they ass" Kutta said as he smiled. "I seen that shit on the news. Good thing I was still laid up in the hospital, so I ain't gotta worry about the law driving down on me. But my cousin told me he be fucking with Stacey" Dewight said. "Alright, so what that mean?" Kutta asked with some aggression in his tone. "Chill out, fool! He finna play her close and see what's what" Dewight said. "Oh, I thought you was about to say he riding with them! I was gone get on his ass!" Kutta said. "Yeah, ight!" Dewight said then started laughing. Kutta started laughing before he hurried and got back serious. "But naw, on some real shit, see if that nigga can get the drop on that nigga Keimon. I know he sent them lil niggas my way" Kutta said. "Come on, man, you know I already hollered at the nigga 'bout that" Dewight responded. "Bet, 'cause we gotta get his bitch ass out the way before he have a mafucka catch one of us. You know his scary ass ain't gone do shit his self" Kutta said. "Why should he if his bitch ass caked up" Dewight said. "Yeah, you right. But he still a bitch!" Kutta said as he got up from the couch and walked to the kitchen. "So, what shit been looking like out here?" Dewight asked. "Shit been rolling, you know, I ran through that shit. I was just waiting on you so you can holla at yo man's. I grabbed like twenty grits of some other shit, just to hold me over" Kutta said. "So, what we finna do grab one or two whole ones?" Dewight asked. "Man, my nigga, with all

48

this shit going on, I think I just wanna grab a hunnit grits and hold on to my lil bread. Just in case shit hit the fan and I need it" Kutta said. "Well, I ain't finna let shit slow my bread down, Imma fuck around and grab five hunnit. But you ain't wrong, a mafucka might need to hold on to some cash right now" Dewight said. Kutta opened the refrigerator, grabbed a bottle of apple juice and sipped from it as he walked back into the living room. "Whenever you ready, I got yo bread at my crib. We can grab that shit and make it happen" Kutta said as he sat back down. "Ight I'mma hit that nigga in about an hour. You ain't got no *gas*?" Dewight asked. "Hell yeah!" Kutta responded. "Man, roll that shit up. My nigga, I need to get high, my mafuckin shoulder hurt" Dewight said. "They ain't give you no pain pills?" Kutta asked.

Dewight's phone started to ring before he could respond. He looked down and see it was Cocoa's number. *I wonder what she want...* he thought to himself before he picked it up. "What up?" Dewight asked. *Hey Dewight, I just seen your dad, and he told me what happened to you. Are you okay?* Cocoa asked "Yeah, I'm good. Where you see that nigga at?" Dewight asked trying to change the subject. *Down here in Beloit, at the gas station*, Cocoa said. "Oh, yeah? That's what's up. I'm good, though, good looking on checking up on me, I appreciate it." Dewight said. *No problem at all. But I'm also calling 'cause I have something that you might be interested in. Well, I know you'll be interested in it,* Cocoa said. "Oh, yeah? What's that?" Dewight asked. *Well, I don't wanna say over the phone. But I can come up that way and show you*, Cocoa said. "Ight, I'm at my crib, just pull up on me" Dewight said. *Alright, I'll be down there in about an hour*, Cocoa said. "Ight,

I'm here" Dewight said. *Okay*, Cocoa said, then ended the call. Dewight put his phone back on the coffee table and looked up at Kutta. "What was we talking about?" He asked. "Shit, my nigga, I don't even remember." Kutta said as he broke down a cigarillo.

Meanwhile

Keef and Denise laid in bed watching TV when Keef's phone started to ring. He reached over to the nightstand and grabbed it. He quickly answered it when he seen it was Scooter's number. "Where you at?" Keef asked as he answered the phone. *I'm outside. You want me to come in or you coming out?* Scooter asked. "You can come in. I'm finna come down and open the door" Keef said. *Say no more*, Scooter said and ended the call.

Keef jumped out of bed and slipped into some gym shorts and ran downstairs. As he walked through the foyer, he could see Scooter standing at the door through the glass door frame. "Come in" Keef said as he opened the door. Scooter walked into the house and stood in the foyer. Keef walked off but stopped when he noticed Scooter wasn't following him. "You good?" Keef asked as he turned around. "Yeah, I'm good" Scooter replied. "Well come in, nigga, why you acting all strange and shit?" Keef asked. "Aww shit, my bad, bro. I ain't know what the hell was going on" Scooter said, as he started to follow Keef. Keef made his way into the living room and sat down on the couch. Scooter followed and took a seat as well. "So, what's good?" Scooter asked. "Shit really. I called you over here 'cause I wanted to holla at you. I ain't had the chance to link with you since that shit happened in Cali" Keef said. "Man, that's my bad, bro. I was drunk as hell" Scooter said. "I know how that shit go, plus you was fresh out. But you my nigga, so I ain't gone sugarcoat shit with you. I hollered at bro and he saying he ain't fucking with you, but he ain't gone leave you out here flicked up. We came too far for that" Keef said as he stood up and walked over to the TV stand and grabbed the stack of cash off it. Scooter sat there shaking his head 'cause he understood Keimon's logic. Keef tossed the stack of cash to Scooter then sat back down on the couch. "That's a hundred Gs. Bro told me to give you that so you can get on your feet" Keef said. Scooter fanned through the stack of hundred-dollar bills. For a split second, he thought about giving it back. He felt like he didn't need no handouts, but quickly changed his mind. "Tell fool I said good looking" Scooter said as it took everything in him to act grateful. "I got you!" Keef replied. "But I got some shit I need to take care of real quick. Imma hit yo line when I get done with that. Good looking out" Scooter said as he stood up. "Ight, bet just hit my line" Keef responded. Scooter walked out of the living room and back to the front door as Keef followed. Keef knew Scooter felt some type of way and he felt bad that he had to be the one to cut Scooter off. He always envisioned them all getting money together, but that shit was short-lived. "Ight, bro" Scooter said as he turned and shook Keefs hand. "Ight, love, bro" Keef said before Scooter walked out the front door.

Meanwhile

Tick pulled up into Stacey's parking lot on Pheasant Ridge Trail, parked his 2017 Dodge Charger and got out. He pulled his phone from his pocket and dialed Stacey's number as he walked up to the building. *Hey*, Stacey said as she answered the phone. "I'm at the building door" Tick said as he stood there. *It's already open. I'm about to unlock the apartment door now*, Stacey said. "Ight" Tick said as he pulled the building door open and walked in. He walked up the stairs to Stacey's apartment. As he walked in, he noticed Stacey sitting at the kitchen table, smoking a cigarette. "You good?" He asked as he closed and locked the door. "I'm alive, but I feel like shit" Stacey said as she exhaled a cloud of smoke. Tick walked into the kitchen and sat down at the table. "Man, I'm sorry to hear about your brothers" he said. "Thank you" Stacey said as she inhaled another cloud of smoke from her cigarette. "I honestly can't fucking believe my brothers are dead. This shit is unreal!" Stacey added. "Yeah, that is crazy. If you don't mind me asking, what the hell happened?" Tick asked—in an attempt to get some information out of her. Stacey sat there quiet for a moment before she looked over at Tick. "They got mixed up with the wrong person" Stacey said as she put her cigarette out. "You know you can trust me. If it's anything you need me to do, just let me know. I got you, Stacey" Tick said. "I know I can trust you. I trust you more than anybody" Stacey said as she stood up and walked over to Tick and sat on his lap. "That's good to hear. 'Cause I'm here to help you with whatever" Tick said as he looked Stacey into her eyes. "Whatever?" Stacey asked him. "Whatever!" Tick replied. "Well, there is something I need your help with" Stacey said as she laid her head on his shoulder. "What's that?" Tick asked. "It's some niggas riding around looking for my brother's killer, but I don't trust that they'll get the job done. So, can you find him and take care of him for me?" Stacey asked Tick, sounding very seductive. Tick sat there quiet for a second, he knew this was his moment to dig up as much information as possible, he wanted to make sure he played his cards right. "So, you know who killed your brothers?" Tick asked. "To be honest, no, I don't… but I do know who it might be" Stacey replied. "Who is that?" Tick asked. "First tell me if you're going to do it for me, then I'll tell you all about it" Stacey said. "I told you. If you need anything, I'll take care of it. I got you, Stacey!" Tick said. "Okay, so this stays between me and you" Stacey said as she stood up and looked at him. "Come on, now, Stacey! This me you talking to" Tick said reminding her that she could trust him. "You right. Well, about a couple of weeks ago, Kutta caught me walking out of my apartment and he forced me back in and robbed me. But the shit he robbed me for wasn't mine, it was Keimon's. Keimon paid my lil brothers to kill Kutta, but they ended up shooting his friend. Then the next thing I know, I got a call from my mom telling me that they were killed. I just know Kutta did it, I'm not a hundred per cent sure, but I feel it in my gut. Now Keimon paid some niggas from Chicago to find Kutta and kill him, but I don't trust Keimon's judgement on this, so I want you to do it. I have thirty thousand dollars saved up. I'll give it to you; I know you might know somebody that could get close to him" Stacey said. "I can do that. I know a little about the nigga Kutta. I think I can get to him. You know I don't want your money. But you gotta promise me that this conversation gone stay between me and you, I ain't trying to go to jail" Tick said. "I promise you it will 'cause I ain't trying to go to jail either. I just want to make sure this nigga get what he deserves" Stacey said. "I got you!" Tick said. "Good" Stacey said, then walked over to Tick and kneeled in front of him. "Well, since you not going to take my money… let me thank you another way" she said before she reached and pulled on the waist band of his sweatpants. "Now, I ain't gone turn this down!" Tick said and laughed before he raised up, allowing Stacey to pull his sweatpants down to his ankles.

Meanwhile

Cocoa pulled into Dewight's parking lot and parked her Lexus. Cocoa and Dewight had met a few years back through his father, so she knew he was someone she could trust. She pulled her phone from her purse and dialed his number. *What up?* Dewight asked as he answered the phone. "I'm outside" Cocoa responded. *Ight, ring the bell and Imma buzz you in,* Dewight said. "Alright" Cocoa said, then she ended the call. She put her phone back in her purse, took the keys from the ignition and got out of her Lexus. As she walked up to the building, she started to think about how fast things had turned around since her robbery and, if everything continues to go as it has been, it won't be long til she'd be living better than she's ever lived before. Cocoa pressed the doorbell and Dewight quickly buzzed her into the building. She walked up the stairs to Dewight's apartment and knocked on the door.

"What's good" Dewight said as he opened the door for her and let her in. "Not much" Cocoa replied. Kutta walked out the kitchen and stopped in his tracks when he seen Cocoa standing there wearing a pair of black Fendi jeans and a white Fendi t-shirt that perfectly hugged her frame. Her Balenciaga sneakers made her look a little taller than she was. Dewight locked the door and hobbled over to the couch and sat down.

"Kutta, this Cocoa, Cocoa this my man's Kutta" Dewight said introducing them to one another. "Hey, how you doing?" Cocoa asked as she walked around the sofa and sat down. "What up?" Kutta said as he stood there. "So, what's good?" Dewight asked Cocoa. "I got something I know you mess around with, and I wanted to see if you wanted to buy it" Cocoa said as she pulled a hundred grams of heroin from her purse and tossed it over to Dewight. "What you want for this?" Dewight asked as he looked at the grams. "Eight thousand" Cocoa responded. "This shit look like some good shit, but I can get this for seven thousand." Dewight said. "But what you getting ain't this" Cocoa said, trying to convince him into buying it. "It might not be, but what I get been working for me, no problems. I don't think it make sense to pay a thousand more than what I'm paying already" Dewight said. "Well, I guess I understand that" Cocoa said. She knew it would sell regardless, but she didn't want to be sitting on it, she figured it was all free money at the end of the day, so what the hell. "You know what, Dewight, I'll take seven thousand for it" Cocoa said. "This all you got?" Dewight asked. "That's all I got on me, but if you want some more, just call me" Cocoa said. Dewight looked over at Kutta who was still standing there checking Cocoa out. "Kutta, you got some cash on you?" Dewight asked. "Yeah, what you need?" Kutta asked. "Just give me half on this so we can see what's to it" Dewight said. Kutta reached into his pocket and pulled out a stack of cash and counted off three thousand five hundred and walked over to the sofa and handed it to Cocoa. Dewight got up from the couch and made his way to the back room. "So, Cocoa why I ain't never seen you before?" Kutta asked. Cocoa chuckled a little before she turned and looked back at Kutta. "Maybe because I'm not from here" Cocoa replied. "Well, where you from?" Kutta asked. But before Cocoa could respond, Dewight hobbled back into the living room. "Here go the other half. Imma have my people check this shit out. If it's some bullshit, Imma need my cash back. If they fucking wit it, Imma need some more" Dewight said. Cocoa sat there nodding her head as she counted the money. "If they say it's some bullshit, I'll bring you your money back, but I know they won't, so I'll be waiting on your call" Cocoa said. "Ight, say no more" Dewight said. "I appreciate it, Dewight" Cocoa said as she stood up. "You know it's all love" Dewight said as Cocoa made her way to the door. "It was nice to meet you, Kutta" Cocoa said as she unlocked the door and opened it. "Yeah, nice to see you too!" Kutta said before Cocoa walked out and closed the door behind herself. Kutta walked over to the door and locked it before he looked out the peep hole. "Folks, how you know her? Tell me you hit that shit?" Kutta asked as he turned around. Dewight started laughing. "You don't miss shit! Naw, I ain't never fucked her, she cool people. That's where we keep it at" Dewight said. "Shit, you better than me. She nice... I can see myself fucking that" Kutta said. Dewight started shaking his head 'cause he knew Kutta was serious about wanting to fuck Cocoa. He couldn't blame him 'cause he wanted to as well. "What you think about this shit?" Dewight asked tossing the hundred grams over to Kutta.

Dewight's phone started to ring as Kutta took his time looking at the grams. He picked his phone up and answered when he noticed it was his cousin Tick. "What up, cuz?" Dewight asked. "Aye, meet me at my crib, ASAP!" Tick said as he drove down Park Street. "Say less, I'm finna be on my way" Dewight replied. "Ight, bet" Tick said, then ended the call. Dewight got up from the couch and looked over at Kutta. "Aye, let's slide over here to cuz crib real quick. I think he got something for us" Dewight said. "Ight" Kutta said before he tossed the grams back to Dewight.

Meanwhile

T-mac sat in the passenger seat with his SD .9mm on his lap as Tuck drove down Allied. T-mac was out for blood because he needed that sixty-thousand dollars Keimon put on Kutta's head. As Toosii's song "Choir" music poured through the speakers, he had his eyes wide open looking for any nigga that resembled Kutta. He reached and turned the music down when his phone started to ring. "What's wrong'?" T-mac asked as he answered the phone. *Where you at? My water just broke!* Ke-Ke said in a panic. "Damn, I'm out of town right now!" T-mac said, frustrated that her water broke while he's out of town. *Well, you need to come home, I'm not finna do this by myself, Mac!* Ke-Ke said. "Ight, shorty!" T-mac said, then ended the call. He was happy to become a father, but he hated who he laid up and had a baby with. "Damn, skud, we gotta find this nigga! This bitch 'bout to have the baby! I need that sixty, bro. I'm finna have a lil boy to look after!" T-mac said. "You finna go back?" Tuck asked. "Hell na! You must ain't just hear me say I need that sixty. I can't miss this bread" T-mac said as he clutched his .9mm on his lap. Tuck made a right turn onto Carling before he looked over at T-mac. "I think you should shoot back down there, then come back after she have the baby" Tuck said. "When I leave, bro, I ain't coming back! I'm finna have to miss this one. I gotta make sure he gone be straight. This lil ten bands ain't shit, bro. I

gotta make a sacrifice for the bigger picture" T-mac said as
they turned onto Verona Road.

Meanwhile

Kutta was itching to find out what it was that Tick had to
say as they walked into Tick's three-bedroom townhouse.
"So, what's good?" Dewight asked Tick as he stood there
holding his crutches. "I just left getting from Stacey crib
getting my dick sucked; but before that shit, the bitch told
me that the nigga Keimon got some niggas down here from
the city looking for Kutta. She tried to pay me to get down
on you, 'cause she don't trust that Keimon's people could do
it. She told me she think you the one that killed her brothers"
Tick said. "Man, that bitch trippin'. I ain't kill her bitch ass
brothers. But now she finna make me kill her ass since she
tryna put some bread on my head" Kutta said. "Look, bro, I
think y'all niggas should lay low until I can figure out who
these niggas is" Tick said, as he had a plan of his own. "I
think if we lay on them niggas long enough, we can hit that
nigga Keimon for some real bread. I got that bitch over there
talking, my nigga! Tick added. "I think we need to get them
niggas out the way, ASAP!" Dewight said. "I feel you, cuz,
but check it. The nigga Keimon holding and the bitch who
told me about the shit y'all took from her; I don't think that's
shit compared to what the nigga really got! If y'all lay low, I
can get the drop on Keimon, and we can take his ass down!
It don't make no sense to kill the nigga and let him die with
the bread! We gotta get something for our troubles" Tick
said.

Kutta stood there thinking for a moment. He agreed with Tick and the fact that they could get some more bread out of Keimon, but he wasn't sure how long that would be, and he needed to make his own money in the process. "I feel you and what you saying makes sense. Imma sit down for a week or two at the most. If we ain't got the drop on the nigga by then, bro, I'm going after the nigga myself" Kutta said. "If I ain't got the drop on the nigga by then bro, he all yours" Tick said.

Chapter Six

* * * * *

One week later

It was 11:30pm on a Friday night and things had been going great for Cocoa. She sold two bricks of the heroin she got from Marsai, and she doubled the amount of money that was taken during her robbery. Her girls were happy and so was she, life was finally going good. Cocoa pulled up to club Aragon's parking lot in Rockford, Illinois, and immediately noticed it was packed with all kinds of different high-end cars. Mostly every nigga in the city who had some money was there. Cocoa quickly found a parking spot and parked her Lexus. "It's packed out here tonight!" Cocoa said as she looked over at Josie. Josie is a beautiful African American bombshell standing at 5'6" and 150 pounds. Her small waist, thick thighs, and natural fat ass was a sight to behold. Josie resembled Meagan Good in a lot of ways. She was born in Rockford, but moved to Atlanta a few years after her and Cocoa started stripping. "Yes, it is packed out here tonight! Let's go in here and enjoy ourselves" Josie said. "Where is Ashley and Jennifer?" Cocoa asked as she scanned the parking lot looking for them. "They right over there" Josie said as she pointed to Ashley's BMW x5.

Ashley was your average white chick as far as her looks go. She stood at 5'5", 120 pounds, blonde with a petite body frame. Ashley is a natural money maker and could go dollar for dollar with the best of them, which made her appealing to every nigga. Jennifer is the type of white girl every nigga wanted. She's 5'3"and 140 pounds, with long jet-black hair; her small waist, breasts and bubble butt were perfect for her frame. Jennifer was also a money maker. She owned multiple businesses in different states. Josie, Ashley, Jennifer and Cocoa all met back when they were all 18-year-olds and worked as strippers in Rockford. Over the years, they've matured together and remained the best of friends. Every time the four of them linked up, they put on a show, and someone if not all four of them would end the night on a full blow-out!

Cocoa got out of the Lexus with her hair in a jet-black bob cut, wearing a tan Gucci shirtdress that showed off every curve of her body. Her dark brown Louis heels complemented her dress and her tan Gucci clutch. Josie got out the passenger side of the car with her hair in square braids pinned up in a bun wearing a teal blue Givenchy tube dress that hugged her perfect frame with a pair of black Givenchy heels. They both walked over to the passenger side door of Ashley's BMW. "This bitch can't find her I.D.!" Jennifer said as she rolled her window down. "I was wondering what the hell was taking y'all so long" Cocoa said as she looked into the car. "Girl, come on, we down here with my people, you don't need no I.D.!" Josie quickly said to Ashley. "Alright, here I come." Ashley said as she started putting her things back into her purse. Jennifer rolled her window up and jumped out the BMW looking amazing with her long jet-black hair curled and hanging over her shoulders wearing a skin-tight all white Prada tank dress and a pair of dove grey Prada heels. Ashley got out of her BMW with her hair pulled back into a high ponytail, wearing a yellow strapless YSL dress and a pair of red Jimmy Choo heels. "Y'all ready to fuck these people club up?" Cocoa asked as she started to walk towards the entrance. Josie led the way into the club and felt like all eyes were on her when she entered as she started to dance to Lil Baby's song "Sum 2 Prove". "Yes, it's packed in here tonight! Let's find a table" Cocoa yelled over the music. "Alright" Josie said as she led the way through the crowd and over to a table in the far corner.

Meanwhile

Scooter walked into club Aragon's wearing a fitted black t-shirt, a pair of dark grey Amir jeans, and all-black Versace sneakers. He walked through the crowd and made his way to the bar and waited on a bartender. As he stood there, he scanned the crowd looking for his cousin who was supposed to meet him there. After Keimon and Keef turned their backs on him, he took the hundred-thousand dollars they gave him down to Rockford and started getting money with his cousin Mike. Mike was well-known throughout Rockford and had been getting money there for years.

"What can I get you'?" the bartender asked Scooter, causing him to turn around. "Yeah, let me get a bottle of Hennessy and a bottled water" Scooter said. "Alright" the bartender said before she walked off to get his bottle. As Scooter waited, he looked up and saw Mike walking through the crowd.

"Aye, Mike!" Scooter yelled out to Mike. Mike was the smooth, plain Jane type. He looked over and noticed Scooter and made his way to the bar wearing an all-black Herm & Jogger with black Balenciaga sneakers. "What up, cuz!" Mike said as he walked up to Scooter and shook his hand. "Shit, my nigga, you know me I'm trying to leave out this club with two bad ass bitches!" Scooter said as he scanned the crowd looking for some prospects. "That's easy, cuz! I'm the man in my city. We leaving with whoever we want!" Mike said.

The bartender walked back over to Scooter and put a bottle of Hennessy and a water bottle on the counter. "That'll be one hundred and fifty-two dollars" she said as she looked at Scooter. Scooter turned around and pulled a roll of cash from his pocket, peeled off two-hundred-dollars, and handed it to the bartender. "Keep the change!" Scooter said then turned around and began to scan the crowd for his victims for the night. "Hey, Mike!" Jennifer said as she walked up to the bar. "Damn, Jennifer, you looking good as hell! Where you been at? I ain't seen you in a long ass time" Mike said as he stood there checking Jennifer out. Jennifer smiled and laughed a little 'cause Mike always knew just what to say to make her day. "Thank you, I've been in California working on the new business I started out there" Jennifer said. "I always admired your drive; you've always been a breadwinner so it don't surprise me that you on top of your shit. But let me say this again, you looking good as fuck! Who you in here with?" Mike asked. "Thank you, Mike!" Jennifer said as she blushed and put her hand on his forearm. "I'm here with my girls Cocoa, Ashley, and Josie, they over there!" Jennifer added as she pointed to their table. "So, who are you here with?" Jennifer asked. "I'm in here with my cousin, Scooter. Aye,

Scooter, this Jennifer, Jennifer this is my cousin, Scooter"
Mike said as he introduced them. "How you doing,
Jennifer?" Scooter asked. "I'm fine. Nice to meet you"
Jennifer replied. "So, what y'all drinking?" Mike asked
Jennifer. "Oh, I was about to order a few bottles of Patron"
Jennifer replied. "Alright. Aye, aye, bartender, let me get
three bottles of Patron, five cups, five bottles of water, and
three Red Bulls" Mike said as he got the attention of the
bartender. "Alright, I got you, Mike" the bartender said
before she walked away to retrieve his drinks.

Meanwhile

Tick made a right turn onto Dayton Street on his way to pick
up Jeannie. Tick and Jeannie met a few days ago at a bar
downtown on State Street. Jeannie is a 4'11", 130 pounds,
27-year-old Cambodian. Unlike most Cambodian women,
Jeannie has an amazing natural hourglass shape that turns
heads wherever she goes. Tick pulled up to Jeannie's house
and parked his 8 series BMW in the driveway. He pulled his
phone from his pocket and dialed Jeannie's number. *Tell me
you not outside*, Jeannie said as she answered the phone.
"Yeah, I'm outside!" Tick replied. *Damn, okay, well, can you
give me a few minutes to fix my hair?* Jeannie asked. "Yeah,
take yo time I'm out here" Tick replied. *Okay, I'll be out in a
couple of minutes*, Jeannie responded. "Ight" Tick replied
before ending the call. He reached into the back seat, grabbed
his bottle of Grey Goose, and refilled his cup that sat in the
cup holder. He turned to put the bottle back on the back seat
when he seen a Lamborghini truck pull into the driveway
next door. "Damn, they fucking shit up in that bitch!" he

said to himself as he watched the truck park. "Never!" he said out loud the moment he noticed a black dude getting out of the truck. He looked a little harder and noticed it was Keef. Realizing he hit the jackpot, he crouched down in his seat trying to make sure that Keef didn't recognize him. He watched as Keef and Denise both walked into their house.

Jeannie walked out of her house and up to the passenger side of the car and jumped in. "I'm sorry, I didn't mean to keep you waiting" Jeannie said as she closed the door. "It ain't no problem, you worth the wait" Tick said as he looked over at Jeannie. "Thank you!" Jeannie said as she laughed. "You looking great too, by the way" Tick said as he put the car into drive and backed out of her driveway.

Meanwhile

Scooter had his eyes locked on Cocoa as he stood next to Mike and watched her dance with Josie. The way her ass moved in that Gucci dress made him want her bad. It was something about her personality and her lively spirit that made him feel comfortable around her, and gave him the urge to want to get to know her more. "Cuz, what you know about shorty?" Scooter asked Mike. "Which one?" Mike asked. "Cocoa, I think that's what she said her name was." Scooter said. "Oh, Cocoa she good people. Imma be honest with you up front, cuz, when I told you I was the man in my city, I meant it. Just so you know, I used to fuck on shorty some years back. I ended up fucking all four of them though" Mike said. "Damn, you fucked all four at the same time?" Scooter asked. Mike started laughing, then he took a sip from his drink. "Now, I was fucking Cocoa first. When we stopped fucking around, I fucked Ashley. I did fuck Josie and Jennifer at the same time" Mike said.

Scooter stood there listening to Mike, but he was fixated on Cocoa and he really didn't give a fuck that Mike had fucked her. "I think I'm finna try and get shorty. I need her on my team" Scooter said. "Do yo thang, cuz. She a good bitch, no bullshit" Mike said. Without a second thought, Scooter walked off and made his way onto the dance floor. Mike looked around for Jennifer and seen that she and Ashley were both sitting at the table, so he made his way over to them. "Y'all good over here?" Mike asked as he shouted a little bit so they could hear him over the music. "Yeah, we doing good" Jennifer replied. Mike sat down next to Jennifer and reached into his pocket. He pulled out a bag of ecstasy pills and pulled one from the bag and popped one into his mouth. "Y'all want one?" he asked. Jennifer looked up at Ashley then to Mike before she said, "Yeah I'll take one."

"Let me get one too. I'm trying to let my hair down tonight!" Ashley said. Mike pulled two pills from the bag and handed each of them one. "Aye, Cocoa, can I get a minute of your time?" Scooter asked as he walked up to Cocoa and Josie. "What you say?" Cocoa yelled out so he could hear her over the music. "I said can I get a minute of your time?" Scooter said as he leaned in and whispered into her ear. "Yeah, you can" Cocoa replied. She already knew where the conversation was headed, she'd noticed Scooter undressing her with his eyes since the very moment he laid them on her. She found it attractive because it showed his interest in her, plus, she found him rather handsome. "So, what's up?" Cocoa asked just as they made it off the dance floor. "Look, I know you don't know me, but I been checking you out all night. It's something about you, aside from how beautiful you are, that's drawing me to you. I wouldn't want to leave this club tonight knowing I could have asked for your number and didn't. So, can I get your number so I can get to know you?" Scooter asked. Cocoa smiled 'cause she found his approach a somewhat sexy and straightforward. She hadn't found anyone in years that she was really interested in, so she figured it wouldn't hurt to give him a chance. "I guess I wouldn't mind getting to know more about you" Cocoa said as she smiled. Scooter pulled his phone from his pocket. "So, what's your number?" he asked. "It's 608-525-3425" she said while Scooter typed it into his contact list.

"Aye, Cocoa!" Mike yelled out and waved her over to the table. Scooter and Cocoa both walked over to Mike, Ashley, and Jennifer. "Hey, Mike, what's up?" Cocoa asked. "You trying to party tonight?" Mike asked. Cocoa started laughing 'cause that was their code for popping a ecstasy pill and she couldn't believe he remembered it. "Yeah, why not!" she replied. Mike pulled the bag of pills from his pocket and handed her one. "You want one, cuz?" Mike asked Scooter. "Yeah, let me get one" Scooter replied. "Where is Josie?" Mike asked Cocoa. "She still on the dance floor" Cocoa said before popping the pill into her mouth and swallowing it.

As the night went on, Cocoa and Scooter spent a lot of time dancing with each other and getting to know one another. Scooter had never popped a pill before, so he was really feeling himself. Around 2:30am, the club ended, and everyone started to exit. Mike walked up to Jennifer and put his arm around her shoulders. "Aye, you should come and spend the night with me" He whispered into her ear. Jennifer started laughing 'cause she was happy Mike wanted to end his night with her. "Alright, let me let my girls know I'm about to leave with you" Jennifer said. "Tight bet, I'm finna go get the car and pull up to the front" Mike said as he walked out the club and made his way over to his Dodge Challenger. Jennifer turned around as Cocoa, Scooter, Josie, and Ashley all walked out the club together laughing. "I'm about to go with Mike" Jennifer said as she pulled Ashley to the side. "Alright, I'll let them know you good. Call me when you make it, so I know you safe" Ashley said. "Alright, I will" Jennifer said and walked away. Mike pulled up to the front of the club and Jennifer jumped in and Mike quickly pulled off.

Scooter walked Cocoa and Josie to Cocoa's Lexus. Josie quickly jumped into the car as Scooter and Cocoa stood outside. "So, I must admit I enjoyed myself here tonight with you" Cocoa said as she looked into Scooter's eyes. "I enjoyed your company too. Maybe we can do this again soon, just me and you" Scooter replied. "I would like that" Cocoa said as she smiled. "Ight, Imma call you. Make sure you drive safe" Scooter replied before he pulled Cocoa in and hugged her. "I will. You drive safe as well" Cocoa said as they broke away from their hug. Cocoa jumped into her Lexus and pulled off.

Meanwhile

The next morning, Jeannie walked into her bedroom with breakfast for Tick. She'd gotten up early and made him something to eat because she felt he deserved it after the way he fucked her last night. "Tick" Jeannie said as she shook him and woke him up. He rolled over and wiped his eyes before he sat up. "I made you some pancakes, bacon, eggs, and toast" Jeannie said as she put the tray on his lap. "Good looking!" Tick replied before he picked up a piece of toast and took a bite from it. "I'll be right back; I forgot the orange juice" Jeannie said as she got up and walked out of the room. Tick immediately started to think about seeing Keef walk into the house next door last night. He needed to make sure that Keef really lived next door cause if he did, he had something planned for him.

Jeannie walked back into the bedroom with a cup of orange juice in her hand and handed it to Tick, then sat down on the bed next to him. "So, how do you like it?" Jeannie asked. "It's good!" Tick said as he dipped his pancake into the syrup and took a bite from it. "Aye, let me ask you something" Tick said. "Okay, go ahead" Jeannie replied. "Last night, I seen a Lamborghini truck next door and I was wondering, do the person who drive that truck live over there?" he asked. "Oh, you're talking about Denise's boyfriend, Keef. Yes, he live there with her. I'm so happy for her, she was so excited when he got out of prison" Jeannie replied. Tick sat there quiet for a moment. "That's a nice car, I never seen one of those in person. That's actually my dream car" Tick said trying not make Jeannie think that the focus of the question was not on Keef, but on the car. "Yes, it is a nice car. I like it as well" Jeannie said. "So, I see we got the same taste" Tick said before taking another bite of his food. "What time is it?" Tick asked before she could respond to his last statement. Jeannie got up from the bed and looked over to her clock in the hallway.

"It's 10:30 am" Jeannie said before sitting back down on the bed. "Damn, I normally wake up earlier than that. I got some shit I need to take care of before twelve" Tick said. He then took another bite from his food and handed Jeannie the tray. "Thanks for the breakfast" Tick added as he hurried and put on his pants and shoes. "No problem. So, when am I going to hear back from you?" Jeannie asked. "I'm going to call you tonight. If you not busy later, maybe we can go out to a movie or something" Tick replied. "I'd like to go out to see a movie" Jeannie said. "Ight, we on, then. I'll call you later" Tick said as he started to walk out of the bedroom.

Meanwhile

Kutta sat in the passenger seat of E.A.'s Dodge Durango SRT as they drove down Park Street. "I got some shit lined up off fisher. I need to catch them before they leave. I had they ass waiting for a minute now" Kutta said to E.A. "Ight, I got you" E.A. said as he exhaled a cloud of smoke and passed the backwood to Kutta. Lil Durk's song "I know" blasted through the speaker as they continued to drive down Park Street. *"My shorties slide in SRT's .45 Glock with extended wings, they gone slide when they off them beans, I ain't gone lie can't be no meme"* Kutta said rapping Lil Durk's lyrics.

"Aye, bro, this black Tahoe truck back here seem like they following us" E.A. said as he looked through his rearview mirror. Kutta grabbed his .45 Glock and checked his side mirror to see how far back the truck was. "Aye, turn right up there on Ridgewood, then make a right on Cypress. If they make both them turns with us, pull over. Imma get down on they ass" Kutta said. "Ight" E.A. said as he grabbed his 9mm and made a right turn on Ridgewood and watched as the Tahoe truck turned with them. "Yeah, I think this might be them niggas. Speed up, turn right up there on Cypress, and let me out and keep going. Meet me up in St. Vincent's parking lot" Kutta said as he raised up in his seat and his heart began to beat fast from excitement. E.A. sped up and made a right turn, quickly stopping to let Kutta out of the car. E.A. pulled off. Kutta ran across the street. The black Tahoe truck turned the corner so fast, their tires were screeching. Kutta popped up from behind a car and let off five rapid shots at the driver's door, causing him to swerve and crash into a parked car. Red immediately popped out the passenger side door like a jack-in-the-box with a FN-15 in his hands and began to return fire, causing Kutta to duck behind the car. "Fuck!" Kutta thought to himself as the shots continued to ring out. He stayed low behind the car as Red let off shot after shot. Red stopped shooting and started to creep up on the car. Completely out-gunned, Kutta knew he had to make his move fast, hearing footsteps getting closer and closer. He popped up from behind the car and let out three shots in Red's direction causing Red to duck. He then sent two more shots towards the truck and took off running in between two houses. Red quickly fired shots at Kutta before he ran back over to the truck and jumped in. "Hurry up and get us the fuck out of here!" Red said to the driver as he banged on the dashboard, pissed. He missed, allowing Kutta to get away.

Meanwhile

Marguerite sat at her kitchen table eating and thinking. For the past few weeks, some things had been bothering her and eating away at her soul. She was dying on the inside and wanted to talk to her boys. Keimon walked into his mother's house and walked through the foyer into the kitchen. "Aye, ma, good morning!" he said, when he seen her sitting at the kitchen table. "Hey, baby, good morning. How you been?" she asked. "I been well, ma. What about you?" Keimon asked. "I been hanging in there" Marguerite said in a somewhat sad tone that immediately caught Keimon's attention. "What's wrong, ma?" Keimon asked as he walked over to the kitchen table and sat down across from her. "I just been trying to work through a few issues from my past" Marguerite said as she took a bite from her food. "What? Something that got to do with pops?" Keimon asked. "No baby, it's nothing to do with your dad. Your mom had skeletons in her closet long before I ever even met your father" Marguerite said. "Skeletons like what?" Keimon asked. "It's hard for me to talk about" Marguerite said as she looked over at Keimon. "Ma, you look like this bothering you a lot, and you know I hate to see you sad or stressed out, so what's up?" Keimon asked.

Tears started to run down Marguerite's cheeks, Keimon reached over and wiped them from her face. "Ma, what's wrong?" he asked again. Marguerite wiped the tears from her face and took a sip from her water. "Back when I was fifteen, I got pregnant. I told my mom and dad, and they flipped out and went crazy on me. When we went to the hospital, we found out I was three months pregnant and past the abortion stage. My mom and dad made me put my baby up for adoption minutes after I had my son. He was snatched from my hands and I never saw him again. I hated my parents for that. I pushed him to the back of my mind trying not to go crazy about it, but lately it's been bothering me" Marguerite said as she continued to cry.

Keimon got up from his seat, walked over to the opposite end of the table and sat next to his mother to console her. "Look, ma, you was young and did what your parents made you do, you can't fault yourself for that. I think if it's bothering you, you should try and find him" Keimon said. "He's 34 years old now. What if he don't want nothing to do with me?" she asked. "Ma, I think if you never try to find him, it'll eat you alive. You can't be afraid of the what ifs, you just gotta cross that bridge when you get there. I think you should find him" Keimon said. "How you get so wise, son?" Marguerite asked Keimon as she wiped the tears. "I am who I am because of you, ma. You're an amazing woman, don't beat yourself up!" Keimon said. "Thanks, I love you so much, baby. I'm going to start looking for him right away" Marguerite said before she leaned over and gave Keimon a hug and a kiss on the cheek.

Meanwhile

Dewight laid in his bed with his leg elevated on a pillow. He flamed up his backwood and started flipping through Facebook on his phone. Tick's name and number flashed on the screen of his phone as it started to ring. "What's the word, cuz?" Dewight asked as he answered the phone. *Man, I got some good news, cuz!* Tick said. "What's that?" Dewight asked. *I got the drop on the nigga Keimon twin brother. The nigga driving Lamborghini truck and some more shit* Tick said. "I ain't know the nigga had a twin" Dewight replied. *Me neither, but shit, I think we should get him. The nigga fresh out the joint driving Lamborghini truck, so I know he in tune with his brother. I want you and Kutta to meet me at my crib so we can plan this shit out*, Tick said. "Ight, say no more, I'm firma link up with bro, then pull up on you" Dewight replied. *Ight*, Tick said, then ended the call.

Dewight took another hit from his backwood and dialed Kutta's number. He waited as the phone rang, and rang... then went to voicemail. He ended the call and dialed the number again. *What up, folks?* Kutta asked as he answered the phone. "Shit! Cuz got the drop on fool twin brother! He want us to link with him, ASAP!" Dewight said. *Ight, shit, where you at?* Kutta asked. "I'm at the crib, pull up on me" Dewight replied. *Ight, give me like twenty minutes, I need to switch cars. I just had a lil situation*, Kutta said. "Shit! What happened?" Dewight asked. *Imma tell you in person, Imma hit you when I'm outside*, Kutta replied. "Ight, bet" Dewight said, ending the call.

Meanwhile

"Girl, wake up!" Josie said as she shook Cocoa to wake her up. Cocoa looked around as she woke up and realized she was in her bedroom. She hadn't been home since her robbery. "Why you up so early?" Cocoa asked Josie. "It's not early, it's 12:30 pm and I didn't come up here to stay in the house all day!" Josie said as she stood there fully dressed and ready to go outside and get the day started. "Okay, girl!" Cocoa said as she rolled out of bed and grabbed her phone, then walked to the bathroom. She walked to the toilet and sat down and started pissing. As she sat there, she checked the messages on her phone. *Good morning, beautiful!* a text read from a number she'd never seen before. "Who is this?" Cocoa immediately texted back before she finished using the bathroom and got up to wash her hands. She sat her phone down on the sink counter and walked over to the shower to turn the water on. "Josie, did you hear from Jennifer this morning?" Cocoa said loud enough for Josie to hear her in the bedroom. "It's the afternoon, and yes, they still in Rockford. They said they'll be up here later" Josie said as she walked over to the bathroom door. Cocoa stood at the sink brushing her teeth when her phone chimed with a text message. She looked down and picked it up. *This Scooter, you gave me the number last night*, the message read. Cocoa smiled after reading it was from Scooter. "Josie, what you think about that nigga, Scooter?" Cocoa asked as she finished brushing her teeth. "He seem like he cool or whatever. He is handsome, y'all kinda cute together" Josie said. "You think so?" Cocoa asked before rinsing her mouth out. "Yeah, I do. Plus, I can tell you like him, I seen y'all last night looking like two ninth graders all in love and shit" Josie said. "Bitch, I ain't in love! I do like the nigga vibe! I think it might actually be some potential there. I ain't been in a real relationship since Vito, I think I'm ready for one" Cocoa said as she picked her phone back up to text Scooter back. *Oh, hey, good morning*, she texted back. "Well, go ahead and give him a try, but don't jump in too fast, learn a little more about him first" Josie said. "Oh, I'm not jumping in headfirst, I'm just saying

I'm willing to take him more serious than I do these other niggas I be using just for some dick" Cocoa said as she began to take off her shorts and shirt. "Okay, bitch, go ahead and get in the shower! I'm ready to go outside. When was the last time you talked to Pudge? I been seeing him on Facebook and I wanna give him some of this pussy while I'm up here" Josie said as she laughed and stood in the doorway. "Bitch, you crazy! I talked to him a few days ago. I'll call him for you later, girl" Cocoa said then jumped in the shower.

Meanwhile

Kutta and Dewight pulled up to Tick's townhouse and parked. Dewight was still trying to wrap his mind around the shootout Kutta just told him he had. He knew by the sounds of it shit was real, and they needed to get Keimon out the way before he got them. They both jumped out of Kutta's rental car, walked up to Tick's door, and rang the doorbell. "Come in!" Tick said as he opened the door and stepped to the side to let them walk in. "Bro, I think I came across something good last night!" Tick said as he closed and locked the door. "Yeah?" Kutta asked as Tick led the way into the living room. "Hell yeah! I found that nigga twin brother. I talked to the bitch Stacey to make sure that the nigga had a brother named Keef and she told me all about how the nigga had just got out and shit" Tick said. "So, what's the plan?" Kutta asked before he sat down on the couch. "Yeah, what you got in mind?" Dewight asked. "Look, I know where the nigga live at. The nigga driving a 2020 Lamborghini truck! Them bitch as niggas caked up! I say we snatch his ass up and have the nigga Keimon pay to get him back" Tick said. "But then what we going to do after that shit? I want the money, don't get me wrong, but I'm trying to kill them niggas. I can't be out here going back and forth with these niggas! Ain't no telling how many niggas they paid to try and smoke my top" Kutta said. "I feel you on that! So, what we you think we should do? I just know we got a stain on our hands if we play this shit right" Tick replied. "I think we should hit him for what he got. If he driving Lam truck, he got some cash! We can take his ass down for what he got and kill him! That'll force the nigga Keimon to come out of hiding to try and find me, then I can get his ass" Kutta replied. "What you think, cuz?" Tick asked Dewight. Dewight sat there for a second, running his hand through his beard thinking. "I think we should stain fool, get what he got and get rid of him. It might be risky trying to hold the nigga ransom, it's too much extra shit that could go wrong" Dewight replied. "Ight, well, I say we catch him or his bitch and walk them into the crib. My lil bitch stay next door to the nigga so I can keep an eye on the nigga from there" Tick said. "Ight, me and my lil man's E.A. going to go in 'cause Wight can't go in. Tick, bro, you can keep the eye out, so I know when it's best to go in. We can bust whatever we get down three ways and Imma hit E.A. out of my cut" Kutta said. "Ight, that's cool. So, when we going in?" Dewight asked. "I think the sooner the better!" Kutta said. "Ight, tonight then!" Tick said. "Say no more!" Kutta said as he rubbed his hands together.

Chapter Seven

* * * *

Keef and Denise were in the middle of dinner at Johnny Delmonico's steak house when Keef pulled a small black box from his pocket and placed it on the table. Denise's heart almost stopped at the sight of the box on the table. *Oh my God, he's about to propose!* she thought to herself while Keef sat still and quiet for a moment before he reached over and placed his hand on top of Denise's. "Baby, I been thinking about this for a couple of weeks now. I been going back and forth with myself debating if this is what's best for us. I do believe it is in our best interest" Keef said. Then he opened the box and slid it across the table to Denise. Denise was eager to see how big the ring was, but her hopes of marriage were instantly diminished when she seen it was a key. "What's this, Keef?" Denise asked disappointed it wasn't a wedding ring. "It's the key to our new house I bought for us!" Keef said with a huge smile on his face. Denise put her head down. "What's wrong? You not happy I bought us a house?" Keef asked noticing Denise didn't look happy. "No. I mean, yes, I am happy, but I'm disappointed 'cause my hopes was just up. I thought you was about to ask me to marry you" Denise said.

Quickly realizing he made a bad decision by putting the key in a box that resembled a wedding ring box, Keef put his hands over his face. "Baby, I'm sorry. Damn I flicked up the mood. I should have thought this through" Keef said. "It's okay, baby!" Denise said, trying to reassure him that he didn't mess up the mood. "Naw, it's not 'cause I don't want you to think that I don't want to make you my wife, 'cause I do. I just want to make sure we had a new place to start over at" Keef said. "I understand, baby. So where is this house at?" Denise asked as she reached across the table and grabbed Keef's hand. "It's in Richmond, Virginia" Keef replied. "Virginia? I don't know, Keef. My family, my friends and my job is here in Wisconsin. I can't just get up and leave" Denise said. "Your family and friends can come visit and you can always come back. As far as a job, me and Keimon building an apartment complex down there, and you can manage the property until you find something else you wanna do" Keef said. "I don't know, Keef, that's a big decision to make so soon" Denise replied. "You don't have to make a decision right now. Just think about it; if worst comes to worst, I'll just sell it or rent it out" Keef said before he picked up his drink and took a sip from it.

Meanwhile

Mike and his best friend, Terrell, were enjoying the strippers Mike ordered. Scooter stood off to the side and watched as Mike and Terrell threw money at the strippers. "Aye, cuz, what up?" Mike yelled over to Scooter as he threw more ones in the air. "I'm good, cuz!" Scooter said as he looked down at his phone waiting for Cocoa's response to his text. Mike walked away from the strippers and over to Scooter. "Aye, cuz, look you ain't going to get the bitch by sweating her, let her breathe. In the meantime, let's enjoy these hoes. I paid a lot of cash to fly these hoes out from Houston" Mike said before he wrapped his arm around Scooter's shoulder and pulled him over to where the strippers were dancing.

Mike grabbed a bottle of Rosé Moet and some more ones and handed those to Scooter. Scooter took the money and the Moet bottle, took a sip from the bottle, and threw some ones in the air. "That's what the fuck I'm talking about!" Mike said to Scooter before he walked over to Strawberry. Strawberry was the baddest stripper there. Her caramel skin glistened from the baby oil and her small waist complemented her fat ass. Mike stood there amazed at how her ass bounced as she twerked to "Face" by PnB Rock. He grabbed some more ones and threw them at Strawberry and smacked her on the ass. "Aye, Scooter, cuz, you gotta come check this fat ass out" Mike said, then turned and looked back to see Scooter walking out the room. "This nigga a sucka!" Mike said to himself then turned around and threw more money at Strawberry.

Meanwhile

Josie, Jennifer, Ashley, and Cocoa were all at Pudge's house with him and a few of his guys drinking, smoking, and playing cards. Josie walked into the kitchen laughing at something Pudge just said. "Your phone ringing" Josie said to Cocoa, then handed her the phone. Cocoa looked at the number and seen that it was Scooter. "Hey, how you doing?"

Cocoa asked as she answered the phone. *I'm good, how yo day been?* Scooter asked. "It's been going good. I'm out with a few friends right now. How about you?" Cocoa asked. *Oh, that's what's up. I'm over here at Mike crib chilling he having a lil kick back with some strippers and shit, but I can't stop thinking about you, so I had to call and see if you would like to go out to eat or something with me tomorrow*, Scooter said. "I don't have too much going on tomorrow, we can go out. What time you got in mind?" Cocoa asked. *How about 7:00 pm?* Scooter said. "Yeah, that's fine" Cocoa replied. "Girl, come on! Is you going to talk on the phone all night or is we going to party!" Jennifer asked Cocoa as she walked into the kitchen. "Here I come!" Cocoa replied. "Well, let me get back out here. Call me tomorrow." Cocoa said to Scooter. *Ight. Enjoy the rest of your night*, Scooter replied. "Alright, you too." Cocoa said, then ended the call. She walked over to the counter, grabbed her drink, and walked out into the dining room. "Cocoa, come be my partner 'cause Josie over here flicking up on purpose so TK and Pudge can win" Ashley said. "Girl, no, I'm not!" Josie said in her defense. "Alright, I will be your partner. Pudge know he can't mess with me on these cards" Cocoa said as she laughed and walked towards the table. "Cocoa, you know you can't play!" Pudge quickly threw out there. "Let's see!" Cocoa said. Josie got up from the table and walked over to stand behind Pudge. Jennifer stood in the living room with LT and Mic-Mic sipping her drink and talking shit while the music played in the background.

Meanwhile

Tick opened the car door for Jeannie so she could get into the car and quickly closed the door behind her. He was happy the movie was over because all he could think about was how much money they were possibly going to get from Keef tonight. Tick already had money, but there was nothing like free money, and the fact that he didn't have to do shit but collect had him excited. Tick jumped into the driver seat and started the car. "How did you like the movie?" Jeannie asked as Tick pulled off. "I thought it was a good movie. I ain't gone lie, at first I thought I wasn't going to like it, but I did" Tick said before he looked down at his Rolex and noticed it was 11:22 pm. "So, what's the plan for the rest of the night?" Jeannie asked. "I think we should go back to your crib, sit back, have a few drinks and see what that lead to" Tick said as he looked over at Jeannie and smiled. "I like the sound of that" Jeannie quickly replied just as Tick's phone started to ring. "Hold on one minute" Tick said before he picked his phone up and answered it. "What up, cuz?" Tick asked. *Shit, cuz I'm just trying to see what time you plan on making that happen?* Dewight asked. "Well, shit, right now I'm out west, but I'm on my way east. Imma call you in like thirty minutes" Tick said. *Ight, bet*, Dewight said, then ended the call. "My bad" Tick said as he put his phone down on his lap. "No, that's fine" Jeannie replied. "I wanna thank you for taking me out, I enjoyed the movie" Jeannie added. "You ain't gotta thank me, I enjoy your company" Tick said. "I'm happy to hear that cause I enjoy being around you too" Jeannie said as she blushed. "Can I sync my phone to your radio? I wanna play my music" Jeannie said. "Yeah, you can" Tick replied. Jeannie synced her phone to the radio and played "Apple

Juice" by Jessie Reyez. She turned the music up, sat back, and enjoyed the ride.

Meanwhile

Keimon and Gabrielle walked into Keimon's condo on North Wabash Avenue. Keimon always dreamed of living the high life. After buying his mother a house, he bought a condo for himself sixty stories up in a high-rise building overlooking downtown Chicago. Keimon closed and locked the door then walked over to the kitchen. "Aye, Gab, you want something to drink?" Keimon asked. Gabrielle walked over into the living room and sat her purse down on the white Italian leather sofa. "Yes, water is fine" Gabrielle said. Gabrielle loved Keimon's condo because the layout plus the black and white reminded her of Keisha's house in the movie *Belly.*

Keimon walked into the living room and handed Gabrielle a bottle of water, then picked up the remote from the coffee table and turned on the 80-inch flat screen that was mounted over the fireplace. Gabrielle kicked off her heels and sat down on the sofa. "You know, out of all your places; I like this one the best! It's just something about being here and seeing this view that makes me so comfortable" Gabrielle said before she took a sip from her bottled water. "Yeah, this was my dream crib. I used to always dream of having me a place like this. So, when I got some money, I went and got it. This place is more from the heart and what the younger me wanted. The other spots are just places to entertain" Keimon said as he walked over to Gabrielle and sat next to her on the sofa.

Gabrielle sat there for a moment then looked up at Keimon. "Stacey's little brothers getting killed has been bothering me lately. I feel like their blood is on my hands" Gabrielle said. "Naw, that shit ain't on you, don't allow it to eat at you. That's just how shit works itself out on the street. You're not to blame" Keimon said as he pulled Gabrielle closer. Gabrielle laid her head on his shoulder. She always felt the safest in his arms. "I know, but I can't help but to feel that way" Gabrielle said. "I understand, but you shouldn't hold on to it. I been doing a lot of thinking lately and I think it's best if I find somebody else and put them in charge of taking care of what I been having you do" Keimon said. Gabrielle lifted her head from his shoulder and looked into his eyes. "Why? What I do wrong?" She asked. Keimon stood up from the sofa and looked down at Gabrielle. "You ain't do nothing wrong, Gab. I just been thinking about life and how I feel like I got everything, yet I'm missing the one thing that makes me happy" Keimon said as he reached into his pocket and got on one knee. "Gab, you that one thing that I'm missing. I wanna give you so much more than this world has to offer. I wanna spend the rest of my life with you, so will you make me the richest man in the world and marry me?" Keimon asked. Gabrielle started crying as she put her hand over her face. "Oh my God, Keimon, are you sure?" Gabrielle asked as Keimon held onto her other hand. "I'm sure! So, what you say?" Keimon asked again. "Yes! Yes, I will!" Gabrielle replied. Keimon grabbed ahold of her ring finger and slid a three-carat diamond ring on it. Gabrielle jumped up from the couch and kneeled down and kissed Keimon.

Meanwhile

Dewight drove down East Washington with Kutta in the passenger seat and E.A. in the back seat. All three were ready for Tick to call and drop the location so they could get this shit over with. Kutta inhaled a cloud of smoke from the backwood Dewight rolled, then passed it over to Dewight. "Aye, fool, how long this nigga gone be? I got some shit I gotta do in about an hour" E.A. asked from the back seat. "The nigga should be calling any minute to drop the location, but ain't no telling how long until we can catch the nigga. We can drop you off if you want us to. I'll go in that bitch by myself!" Kutta replied. "On BD, you got me fucked up! I'm getting in on this shit. I ain't firma miss this shit for nothing, I'm just trying figure out if I'm finna have to cancel this shit" E.A. said as he grabbed the backwood from Dewight. "Gone head and cancel that shit 'cause ain't no time limit on this shit" Kutta replied. "Bro, you gone make me fuck you up!" E.A. joked. "Nigga, I ain't worried!" Kutta said as he laughed. Dewight's phone started to ring in the cupholder so he turned the music down and picked it up. "What's the word?" Dewight asked. *Man, cuz, I'm at shorty crib right now, the nigga truck ain't out there and I don't think nobody in the house yet either. The address is 2525 East Dayton Street, it's a yellow house in the middle of the block*, Tick said. "Ight bet! We on it! we finna go over there and camp out for a while" Dewight replied. *Ight, Imma call you if anything change*, Tick said. "Ight" Dewight replied and ended the call. "I got the location now. Imma drop y'all off and let y'all camp over there until the nigga get there. Imma pull around the corner and wait on y'all niggas" Dewight said to Kutta and E.A. Kutta pulled his Ruger .9mm from his waist and cocked the pistol, making sure he had one in the chamber. E.A. picked up his pistol version of SIG's short, barreled rifle from the seat and sat it on his lap. "Let's get this pussy ass nigga!" E.A. said as he rolled the window down and threw the rest of the backwood out the window.

Meanwhile

Keef and Denise pulled out of the High Noon Saloon parking lot and made a right turn onto East Washington, then a right turn into the BP gas station. Keef threw the car into park and turned the music down. "You want something out of here?" Keef asked. "No, I'm fine" Denise said as she sat there drunk off the many long islands she just enjoyed as they shot pool. "Night" Keef said as he jumped out of his truck and walked into the gas station. "Hey, how much that truck cost?" the cashier asked Keef as he walked past the register. "To be honest, I don't know, I got it as a gift" Keef said as he walked to the coolers in back of the store. "That's a nice truck!" the cashier said as he looked out the window at the truck. Keef grabbed a Red Bull and a bottled water and walked up to the register. "Thanks" Keef said as he placed the Red Bull and water on the counter. The cashier quickly rung him up. "That'll be six fifteen" the cashier said. "Ight!" Keef replied before he reached into his pocket and pulled out a roll of cash and handed the cashier a ten-dollar bill. Keef's phone started to ring in his pocket, so he pulled it out and answered it. "What up, bro?" Keef asked as he answered. "Thanks!" Keef said to the cashier as he grabbed his change and walked out the store.

Bro, I'm 'bout to get married! Keimon said happily. "Yeah? Who you finna marry?" Keef asked. *Gabrielle!* Keimon happily replied. "Damn, bro, that's what's up!" Keef said as he walked to his truck. "Man, I fucked up today!" Keef added. *Why you say that? What you do?* Keimon asked. "Man, bro, I gave Denise the keys to our new house in a box that looked like I was about to propose to her and when she seen it was a key, she was pissed 'cause she thought I was about to propose" Keef said as he stood outside of his truck. *Yeah, bro, you gotta make it up to her and ask her to marry you when she least expects it*, Keimon said. *But let me get back in here to Gab. Imma call you tomorrow. Love bro!* Keimon added. "Ight, love bro." Keef said, ended the call, and jumped back into his truck.

Denise sat in the passenger seat rocking her body side to side as she listened to "Love Cycle" by Toosii. "I see this yo shit! This like the fifth time you played it tonight!" Keef said as he put the car into drive and pulled out of the gas station. "Yes, this is my jam, I love this song!" Denise said before she started to sing the lyrics out loud. Keef laughed as he drove up East Washington, he looked over at Denise as she danced in her seat and in that moment, he knew she was the one he wanted to grow old with. Keef made a left turn onto North Street. followed by a right turn on East Dayton Street.

Meanwhile

Kutta and E.A. each laid in the bushes on opposite sides of Keef's porch ready for the moment he rolled up. E.A. looked up and seen head lights coming from the direction on his side of the house and got excited. He was quickly disappointed as he watched the car pass by the house. On the opposite side of the house, Kutta fumbled with his .9mm as his knees began to ache from kneeling in the bushes for so long. *Where the fuck this bitch ass nigga at?* Kutta thought to himself as he leaned back on the house siding a little to stretch his legs. He looked up when he heard music coming from up the street. *Man, I hope this is this bitch ass nigga!* Kutta thought to himself as he pulled his mask over his face. A black Lamborghini truck pulled into the driveway and parked. Kutta watched as Denise and Keef leaned in and kissed each other before Keef turned the truck off and jumped out. Denise jumped out of the passenger side and walked around to Keef and wrapped her arm around his. E.A. sat in the bushes quietly waiting for Keef and Denise to walk onto the porch. "Aye, I love you!" Keef said to Denise as he kissed her on the forehead before they both started walking up the porch stairs.

Keef put his key into the lock, but before he could twist it and unlock the door E.A popped up from the bushes and pointed his SIG at Keef and Denise. "Bitch ass nigga, if you move or get loud, Imma fill yo ass with this hot shit!" E.A. said as he stood in the bushes. Keef and Denise both jumped at the sound of E.A.'s voice. Kutta rushed up on to the porch and grabbed Keef by the back of his shirt and placed his .9mm to the back of his head. "Open the fucking door!" he ordered Keef. "Bitch, get over here" Kutta added as he pointed his pistol at Denise. Denise quickly walked over and stood next to Keef as he unlocked the door. "Look man, you can take whatever you want, just don't hurt us!" Keef said as he pushed the door open. Kutta pushed both Keef and

Denise into the house while E.A. jumped from the porch and rushed into the house closing the front door behind him. "Please, just take what you want and go!" Denise said. "Shut up, bitch!" E.A. said as he smacked Denise with his SIG, knocking her to the floor. Denise covered her face as she cried out. "Man, what the fuck!" Keef yelled as he tried to rush over to E.A. but was quickly stopped in his tracks as Kutta grabbed him and slammed him to the floor. "Where the fuck is the money at?" Kutta asked as he pointed his .9mm down at him. "It's upstairs in the bedroom, in the closet. It's in a Nike shoe box" Keef replied. "Take that bitch upstairs and grab that!" Kutta ordered E.A. E.A. grabbed Denise by her hair and pulled her to her feet. "Come on, bitch!" E.A. said as he snatched Denise to her feet and pushed her towards the stairs. "Man, bro, chill out… she ain't did shit!" Keef said to E.A. as he laid on the floor. Kutta reached down and patted Keef's waistline. "Shut the fuck up and roll over" Kutta said as he pulled Keef's shirt forcing him to roll over onto his stomach. "Keimon yo brother, huh? It's crazy you look just like that bitch ass nigga!" Kutta said, then started laughing.

Keef didn't say anything. He just laid there hoping Denise was okay upstairs. "Bitch ass nigga, answer me when I'm talking to you" Kutta said before he kicked Keef in his ribs. Keef let out a loud grunt before he rolled over on to his side. "Now where the fuck is yo phone at?" Kutta asked. "My pocket!" Keef quickly said as he held his side. E.A. dragged Denise down the stairs and pushed her to the floor next to Keef. Kutta reached down and pulled Keef's phone from his pocket. "I got the bread!" E.A. said as he opened the shoe box and showed Kutta it was stuffed full of hundred-dollar bills. "How much in there?" Kutta asked Keef as he flipped through Keef's phone looking for Keimon's number. "It's one hundred and thirty thousand dollars in there!" Keef replied. "Good! Now get yo ass up!" Kutta ordered Keef as he pointed his .9mm at him. E.A. quickly reached down and snatched Keef to his feet. "What, you think I won't treat you like a bitch too?" E.A. said as he pressed his SIG into Keef's ribs. Kutta found Keimon's number in Keef's phone and called him on FaceTime. "What up, bro?" Keimon asked as he answered the FaceTime call. "Who the fuck is this?" Keimon said as soon as he recognized it wasn't Keef. "This the boogie man!" Kutta replied as he laughed. "Check it out. I got your bitch ass brother right here and his fine ass bitch. Hold on real quick, I think he wanna say something to you" Kutta said as he turned the camera towards Keef and Denise. "Bro, you good?" Keimon asked as he started to panic. "Yeah, bro, I'm good!" Keef said in shame. "For now! Only for now" Kutta said as he turned the camera back to himself. "Word on the street is you put some cash on my head! Well, pussy ass nigga, go and get yo cash back 'cause I ain't dead!" Kutta said as he pulled his mask from his face so Keimon could see him. "Fuck! Bitch ass nigga, Imma kill you!" Keimon said as he slammed his hand on his kitchen counter. "Yeah, yeah, yeah… but in the meantime, you gotta check this out!" Kutta said as he turned the camera back towards Keef and Denise. He focused on both of them, then shot Keef in his face. As Keef laid there, he shot Denise in the head, then emptied his clip into both of them. He started laughing before ending the call. "Let's get the fuck out of here!" Kutta said before he and E.A. rushed out of the house.

Chapter Eight

* * * * *

Ten days later

T oday, we're here to celebrate the lives of both Denise Smith and Keef Evans, as they begin their transition into the afterlife of eternity. To be absent from the body is to be present with the Lord. Amen." the Pastor said as he stood in front of both Keef's and Denise's caskets. Keimon stood in the back of the church and watched as Denise's parents and his mother sat next to each other crying. He couldn't escape the reality that Keef's blood was on his hands because he didn't fill Keef in on what was truly going on. Payback was now at the center of his thoughts. All he wanted was to watch the life drain from Kutta's body as he begged for his life.

"Baby, you okay?" Gabrielle asked before she placed her hand on Keimon's shoulder. Keimon looked over at her and nodded his head, then looked back to the front of the church at both Keef and Denise's pictures. He then directed his gaze to their closed caskets. *I want his casket closed!* Keimon thought to himself, reminiscing on the words he said about Kutta, and now he's here, standing before his brother's closed casket. His blood began to boil as his stomach fell to the floor. He wanted revenge bad. "Baby, let's go sit down" Gabrielle said to Keimon, bringing him back to reality. "Alright" Keimon said, but when he took his first step, his knees buckled and caused him to stumble. Gabrielle grabbed Keimon and led him to the nearest chair so he could sit down. "Are you sure you're okay?" Gabrielle asked again. "Yeah, yeah, I'm good, baby" Keimon said before he stood up. He and Gabrielle both walked up to the front row and took a seat next to his mother.

"I can't believe my baby gone!" Marguerite said as she looked over at Keimon and started sobbing even harder before she placed her head onto his shoulder. "I know, ma! It's going to be okay!" Keimon said in an attempt to comfort her. "Who would want to kill my baby, he just got out?" Marguerite cried out. "I don't know, ma, but I will get to the bottom of it!" Keimon replied as he couldn't help but feel like shit because he knew this was all his fault. Seeing Keef and Denise both get gunned down really ate at his soul. Denise's parents both stood up and walked up to Denise's casket, leaned on it, and started crying. Keimon couldn't take no more; he'd seen enough. "I'll be outside, ma" Keimon said then got up and walked away. Marguerite wiped her tears from her eyes with her tissue, then managed to stand up from her seat and walked over to Keef's casket. "Baby, I'm sorry! I wish I could turn back the hands of time, I'd trade places with you. My soul hurts. I was forced to abandon one child, now I have to bury another one. God, why?" Marguerite asked before she laid her head on Keef's casket and cried out. Gabrielle got up and walked over to Marguerite and placed her hand on her back trying to comfort her.

Meanwhile

It was hotter than it had ever been in Madison and the police were on the manhunt for Keef and Denise's killer. After committing two double homicides in a two-month period, Kutta was nervous and decided he needed to get away. Two days after killing Keef and Denise, Kutta, Dewight, Tamron, and Alyssa all jumped on a flight to Turks and Caicos. Kutta and Dewight sat on Beach Enclave on the deck of their private beach front villa, sipping on strawberry margaritas, while Tamron and Alyssa stood in the ocean facing kitchen, talking and sipping strawberry margaritas as well. Tamron is a 27-year-old mixed German and African American beauty. Her golden-brown skin tone, sandy brown hair and her green eyes were enough to have Kutta eating out of the palm of her hand. Tamron's body was banging at 5'5" and 135 pounds. Her petite frame was to die for, but the flower tattoo that wrapped from her left ankle all the way up her thigh and covered the side of her ass drove Kutta crazy and she knew just how to flaunt it. Her best friend Alyssa is a 29-year-old African American bombshell that resembles model Danielle Herrington to a tee! From her perfectly brown skinned tone, down to her petite body frame. Her yellow and black snakeskin print swimsuit had her looking like she was getting ready to do a photo shoot.

"Aye, Tamron check it out real quick!" Kutta yelled out to her. Tamron walked out on the deck wearing a two-piece yellow and black high waist Versace swimsuit. "What's up?" Tamron asked before she took a sip from her drink. "What y'all got planned for today?" Kutta asked. "Well, Alyssa wanna go snorkeling so it's either that or we can go kite boarding" Tamron replied. "Ain't no either! Today we going snorkeling, end of the story!" Alyssa said as she walked out on to the deck looking like an Egyptian goddess. Dewight looked up and laughed. "End of story, huh?" he asked. "Yes! We been down here five days now and we still haven't went snorkeling! Plus, I already made the reservation with eco tour, so get ready. We gotta be there in an hour" Alyssa replied. "Ight, well, as long as they giving us life jackets I'm wit it" Kutta said before he took another sip from his drink. "A life jacket? What, you can't swim?" Alyssa asked. "Yeah, I can swim, just not for a long time. I get tired fast as hell, plus I been drinking. I ain't tryna die down here" Kutta replied. "Shit, Imma need a life jacket too!" Dewight said as he got up from his beach chair. "Well, I know you need one!" Alyssa said as she laughed and looked over at Dewight. "Oh, damn that's what you on?" Dewight asked as he stopped in his track. "No baby, I'm just joking, you know I love you!" Alyssa replied then she ran over to Dewight and hugged him. "You don't love me... you just love my doggy style!" Dewight said before he slapped her on the ass. "Yeah, I love that too." Alyssa said in a real seductive tone. "Ight, I got you later on!" Dewight said. "Okay, now y'all doing the most!" Tamron said before she took a seat in the beach chair next to Kutta.

Meanwhile

Scooter pulled into the parking lot of the funeral home and parked his car. He looked up and seen Keimon walking over to his Mercedes Benz G wagon. He hadn't seen Keimon since the night he got out of prison, which was over three weeks ago, so he hurried and got out of his car. "Aye, Keimon!" Scooter yelled out to him. Keimon looked up and seen Scooter, then stopped and waited for him to walk up. "Man, bro, how you doing?" Scooter asked. "I'm managing, bro. Good looking on coming out and showing bro some love" Keimon replied. "You know that was my nigga, when I heard that bro was killed, I threw up everything I ever ate" Scooter said. Keimon stood there for a moment and just shook his head 'cause he really didn't know what to say. "You know who did this shit?" Scooter asked. Keimon looked him directly into his eyes and nodded. "Who did it, bro? I wanna make his ass pay for this shit" Scooter said in a low pitch tone. "No, bro, this one on me. I gotta take care of it! If I let somebody else do it, it won't mean shit" Keimon replied. "My nigga, at least let me know who the fuck did this" Scooter said. "I don't think you know this nigga. When I came back to Madison after college, the nigga was new to Madison from Chicago. A dark-skinned nigga named Kutta. He be fucking with them niggas that be out west. Trust me, Imma handle this" Keimon said. "Man, bro, I can't believe this shit" Scooter said. "Me neither!" Keimon replied.

Gabrielle walked out of the funeral home to check up on Keimon. When she made it to the parking lot, she scanned around looking for him. She started walking in his direction when she noticed he was standing over by his truck talking to Scooter. "Hey, how you doing, Scooter?" Gabrielle asked as she walked up and wrapped her arm around Keimon's arm. Scooter looked down and noticed she had a big ass wedding ring on her ring finger which caused his stomach to drop. "I'm great. How you doing?" Scooter asked. "I'm fine" Gabrielle replied before she looked over at Keimon. "You okay, baby?" Gabrielle added as she looked up at him. "Yeah, I'm good. I'll be back in there in a minute I just needed some air" Keimon replied. "Okay. I love you." Gabrielle said then she kissed him. "Love you too" Keimon said before he looked over at Scooter who awkwardly stood there watching. He already knew how Scooter felt about Gabrielle. "Okay. It was good to see you again, Scooter" Gabrielle said before she started to walk away. "Yeah, same to you" Scooter replied as she walked away. Scooter waited until Gabrielle was out of ear shot before he spoke again. "Y'all finna get married?" Scooter asked. "Yeah" Keimon replied, sensing the hate coming from Scooter. "Man, that's what's up! We gotta link up and celebrate that!" Scooter said. Keimon looked at him 'cause he couldn't believe he had the audacity to ask him to celebrate with him knowing damn well he was hating. What Scooter didn't recognize was that Keimon was steps ahead of him and could see him coming with some bullshit from miles away. "Imma have to pass on that, bro. I got more important shit I gotta attend to right now, but maybe somewhere down the line" Keimon replied. Keimon's rejection to Scooter's offer was a blow to his pride and made him feel like Keimon really thought he was better than him. "Ight, bet. But let me get up in here and pay my respects to bro." Scooter said before he walked away. *Imma bring that bitch ass nigga down off that high horse* Scooter thought to himself as he walked through the parking lot.

Meanwhile

Vito walked up to the phone and dialed Cocoa's number. He sat there as it rang and waited on her to accept the call. *All calls are subjected to monitoring and recording. You may began speaking now*, the automated system said. "Hello" Vito said as Cocoa answered. *Hey, baby! How you doing? Why I haven't heard from you in over two weeks?* Cocoa asked. "I'm good, I just been chilling. Sometimes I gotta take some time to get my mind right. It be fucking me up sometimes knowing I'm going to die in here" Vito replied. Cocoa intended on chewing him out, but after hearing his response, she changed her tone. *Baby, you can't think like that cause it'll only stress you out*, she replied. "Yeah, I know that's why I haven't called. I'm good, now it just be a battle within myself, but it ain't nothing I can't overcome!" Vito said trying to reassure her that he was good. "But thanks, I got the money and the pictures you sent me. I see you out there looking good as hell. Aye, the picture with you and the Puerto Rican chick in it, who is that?" Vito asked. *Which one?* Cocoa asked. "The one with you in the red skirt with the white top and ole girl got on a blue dress." Vito replied. *Oh, that's one of my girls. Her name is Marsai. Why you ask?* Cocoa asked. "Just asking!" Vito replied. *No, you not just asking! Don't get fucked up, Vito*, Cocoa said. "Knock it off!" Vito said as he started to laugh. *Ain't shit funny, Vito, you better stop playing with me!* Cocoa said letting Vito know she was jealous that he was showing interest in someone else. "But how you doing? How life been out there?" Vito asked. *I been doing good; things been going well. I been trying to buy a house*, Cocoa happily replied. "Oh yeah? Where at?" Vito asked. *I got my eye on one in Madison. I really like it, it's a three bedroom two and a half bath with a two-car garage and a nice backyard*, Cocoa replied. "How much they asking for it?" Vito asked. *They want three-hundred and twenty-five thousand, but I have a hundred thousand in the bank that I been saving over the years and I was approved for a two-hundred and fifty thousand dollar loan from the bank, so I'm just hoping I get that house*, Cocoa said. "Damn, I like hearing that you doing yo thang. That makes me proud of you and let me know everything I taught you wasn't in vain" Vito said. *No, it wasn't, I've always listened to what you said and I often think about what you taught me. I am who I am because of you. But speaking of what you taught me, I have to tell you something…* Cocoa said then paused for a moment. "What's that?" Vito asked. *Well in the spirit of being real and always be true to myself, I want you to know I met this guy a little over a week ago. We went out a few times, I didn't fuck him, but I do like him enough to know I want to be with him. I've always said if I was to find someone, I was serious about, I would tell you. Now, no one will ever have my heart like you do, and no one could ever make me stop talking to you. I just feel like I have to tell you how I'm feeling*, Cocoa replied.

Hearing that Cocoa found someone that she was willing to take serious hurt more than hearing the judge give him a life sentence. Vito refused to let Cocoa know that, plus he knew he couldn't have her, and he'd honestly rather see her happy. "I think you should pursue it and see what happens. You only get one life to live and I'd rather see you happy before I ever try and hold you back" Vito said. *Are you sure?* Cocoa asked. "Yeah, see what's to it. Just don't disappear on a nigga" Vito replied. "I will never leave you in there alone. Me pursuing him don't change anything between me and you. It ain't no nigga in this world more important to me than you are,

Vito." Cocoa said. Vito heard her, but he couldn't really put any trust in her words. After a life of betrayal, it wasn't easy for him to take a person's words at face value. "Damn, it just beeped, we got a minute left. But, look, Imma call you back in a few days. I mean it when I said what I said if it makes you happy, it makes me happy" Vito said. "I love you, Vito" Cocoa said. "Love you too" Vito replied, then ended the call.

Back in the Caribbean

After snorkeling and enjoying some Pad Thai cooked up by a master chef, Kutta and Tamron went to their room to have some private time and enjoy their ocean front view. Kutta stood sipping on a glass on Cognac as he looked out at the ocean. So much had happened in the past few months, so being able to relax and not have to worry about looking over his shoulder was peaceful. He drifted off into another world as he stared out into the ocean. Tamron walked out of the bathroom wearing a white robe with her curly sandy brown hair pinned up in a bun. She walked over to the nightstand and synced her phone to the radio and played "Shame" by Summer Walker. She looked over at Kutta who was staring out at the ocean. She loved the way the stars lit up the sky and how the reflection from them bounced off the ocean. Tamron knew even though Kutta wouldn't make their relationship official, she was his number one, and that there was nothing he wouldn't do to make her happy. She loved him dearly for being her peace. She got up from the bed and walked over to Kutta and placed her hand on his shoulder, causing him to snap back to reality. Kutta looked over his shoulder and seen Tamron's beautiful face, he loved staring into her eyes because he could see her soul, which was a loving and peaceful sight. "You know you sexy as hell, right?" He asked. Tamron smiled because he knew just what to say to make her feel as beautiful as she looked. "I know now, 'cause you make sure I do" she replied as she stared into his eyes. "You know I love you!" she quickly added. "Yeah, I know now, 'cause you make sure I do." Kutta replied being funny.

Tamron laughed a little cause she knew he was trying to be funny which was just what she loved the most about his personality. Kutta took a sip from his cognac then leaned in and kissed Tamron. "Yeah, I know you love me. I love you too!" Kutta said as he turned to face her and pulled her closer to him. He always enjoyed how wonderful she smelled. Tamron placed her chin on his chest and looked up at him. "Thanks for bringing me out here, I really needed this" Tamron said as she looked up at him. "Thank you for putting me up on this shit. I ain't never did this before, I'm enjoying this shit" Kutta replied "Well, you know I don't mind putting you up on game which is very often!" Tamron said before she started laughing.

Kutta looked down at her and her pearly white teeth and pink lips made him want to kiss her again, so he grabbed her chin and kissed her before kissing her another time. He really couldn't get enough of her beauty, but her personality made her shine brighter than the oil glossed over her golden-brown skin. Tamron grabbed ahold of Kutta's tank top with both hands and pulled him towards the bed. Kutta quickly followed her and watched as she crawled onto the bed, never looking away from him. It was something about Tamron that drove Kutta crazy and he loved the feeling of it. Kutta watched as Tamron unwrapped her robe and allowed it to fall down from one of her shoulders. She placed her feet flat on the bed and opened her legs up as she bit her bottom lip. "Damn!" Kutta said as his dick began to grow in his shorts. He gulped the rest of his drink and placed it on the nightstand. He walked closer to the bed and grabbed a hold of Tamron's legs; her skin was so soft and silky smooth which was another thing on a long list of reasons why he loved her. He slowly ran his hands down her legs before he aggressively pulled her closer to the edge of the bed. "Ooh shit!" Tamron said as she laughed a little. She loved how gentle, yet aggressive Kutta could be. Kutta crawled between her legs then leaned down and gently kissed her on the lips. He then gradually moved down to her neck as he delicately ran his tongue up her neck back up to her ear softly biting the bottom of her ear before gently sucking on it while breathing softly into it. He raised up and pulled her robe open and slowly ran his hand from the center of her chest down to her stomach. "Damn, I love how soft your skin is" he said before he grabbed one of her breasts with his other hand. He leaned over and softly ran his tongue around her areola before he started to suck on her nipple. "Shit!" Tamron moaned as she reached up and ran her hand over his head. Kutta softly began to kiss and lick down the left side of her stomach before he ran his tongue across her waistline down to the center of her stomach. He reached down to her already wet pussy and began to rub his fingertips over her love button.

Kutta went down and began to kiss her inner thigh before he made his way up to her pussy. He first kissed it to show his appreciation to it before he went in and began to lick along the outside of her second set of beautiful lips. With one hand, he spread them open, slowly and softly dipping his tongue in to get a taste of her sweetness. "Oh shit" Tamron moaned as she put her head back already knowing Kutta was about to destroy her pussy until she reached climax multiple times. Kutta wasted no time going in for the kill and started to devour her pussy as if it were a steak and he hadn't eaten in months. He sucked and licked on her pussy for over ten minutes. Three orgasms later, he flipped her over and slowly slid into her soaking wet pussy. He began to stroke her from the back. "Kuttaaaaa, yes, baby, this is your pussy!" Tamron moaned as Kutta pounded harder and harder with each stroke. "Damn, this pussy good as fuck!" Kutta said before he slowed down, and smacked Tamron's ass then instantly picked up the pace and started to pound her. "Right there! Please, don't stop, please! Yes, Kutta just like that! I'm about to cum…!" Tamron yelled out before she reached climax. Kutta continued to pound Tamron's pussy as she started to run from him. He grabbed ahold of her waist so she couldn't get away. Kutta started to pace himself by speeding up and slowing down. He fucked her from the back for over twenty minutes before Tamron reached another climax. Kutta quickly followed Tamron and exploded inside of her before he fell over on the bed.

Chapter Nine

* * * * *

Two weeks later

It had been two weeks since Cocoa and Scooter made their relationship official. Cocoa was finally happy—even though they were still in the honeymoon phase of their relationship—she knew he was the one. She enjoyed his company and the way he made her feel. He wasn't Vito, but he would do. Scooter and Cocoa drove down 1-94 on their way back to Beloit from Rockford. Scooter had talked Cocoa into putting some money with him and getting their dope from his cousin Mike. Scooter wanted Cocoa to focus more on her escort business and let him worry about hustling and the streets. Cocoa seen that as a win-win for herself, so she and Scooter both put dollars each into the pot and went down to Rockford and grabbed four bricks of heroin.

As they drove, Cocoa quickly turned the music down when she heard her phone ringing in her purse. She reached in then pulled it out and looked at the number, she answered when she noticed it was Marsai. "Hey, Marsai. How you doing, girl?" she asked as she answered the phone. *I'm doing fine. I'm calling you 'cause, girl I'm ready to get back to work!* Marsai replied. "Alright, I'll put your ad back up as soon as I get back to Beloit" Cocoa happily said because Marsai was a major money maker and with her back, things were going to pick up which meant more money for her. *Alright, just call me when you get back*, Marsai replied. "Okay girl, I will!" Cocoa said before she ended the call. She looked up at Scooter as he drove up the interstate. "When we get back, take me to my car before we go home" she said. "Ight" Scooter replied as he continued to drive up 1-94. "After I'm done putting this shit together, you wanna go out to eat?" Scooter asked. "Yeah, I would like that" Cocoa replied. "Ight!" Scooter said as he reached over and put his hand on Cocoa's thigh. Cocoa looked over at him and smiled as she put her hand on top of his.

Meanwhile

Keimon walked into the apartment behind T-mac and locked the door. He turned and walked into the living room where T-mac and Red both stood watching Tuck and TK playing the PS4. Keimon was tired, stressed out, and hellbent on revenge. He wanted to make sure T-mac knew he was serious about getting Kutta. "What up, skud?" Red asked when he turned around and seen Keimon standing there. "Shit, I came through to holla at y'all" he replied. "I almost had the nigga the one time I did see him, but he got away" Red said. "That's why I'm here to holla at y'all, we got a change of plans. I don't want y'all to kill him, I want y'all to kidnap him. I wanna kill that nigga myself. He killed my brother, so I gotta be the one to kill him" Keimon replied. "Ight, so do the price change?" T-mac asked 'cause he still needed to get that money to take care of his seed. "Yeah, the price gone change, it just doubled! Twenty thousand up front and two-hundred thousand for y'all niggas to split how you see fit once you bring me this nigga" Keimon replied. "Ight, we on it!" Red said excitedly, then inhaled a cloud of weed smoke and passed the blunt over to T-mac.

Keimon walked around and sat down on the couch next to Tuck. "I need to see this bitch nigga bleed and beg me for his life!" Keimon said as he looked around the room. "We got you, bro!" T-mac replied. "Y'all can't have me, bro, y'all still sitting around playing the game and shit!" Keimon said, getting angry. T-mac and Red looked over at each other surprised at how Keimon was talking at them. He was lucky that he was Von's cousin because they both would have got on his ass, but the fact that he just doubled the price made T-mac and Red both give him a pass. "You right! Man, get y'all asses up and let's get out of here and find this nigga!" T-mac said to Tuck and TK before he walked to the back to grab his pistol. Keimon put his hands over his face and let out a deep sigh, he was stressed to the max and short tempered, but he couldn't relax until Kutta was in the dirt.

Meanwhile

Dewight, Tamron, Alyssa, and Kutta pulled up to Tamron's house after three weeks in the Caribbean. Kutta and Dewight knew they had to get back to business. Dewight put the car into park before they all jumped out. Kutta and Dewight grabbed Tamron and Alyssa's bags and walked them to Tamron's door. "Thank you again!" Tamron said as she turned to face Kutta. "You welcome! I had a nice time with you" Kutta replied. "Ight, shorty!" Dewight said as he gave Alyssa a hug. "Whatever, big dude! When am I going to see you again?" Alyssa asked. "Just call me" Dewight replied. "Alright" Alyssa said before she picked her bags up and walked into Tamron's house. Kutta leaned in and kissed Tamron. "Imma see you soon!" Kutta said as he broke away from their kiss. "Okay. I love you" Tamron replied. "I love you too, shorty!" Kutta said before he walked off the porch and back to Dewight's car. He jumped in and closed the door then looked around. "Man, bro, I hate that we had to come back to this shit. We gotta hurry up and get to my crib so I can grab my joint. I can't let these niggas catch me lacking" Kutta said. "Man, I feel you. We need to grab some move too. I tricked off too much cash out there" Dewight replied. "You? Shit nigga we both did that, but all that shit was on Keimon" Kutta said before he started laughing. "Yeah, you right!" Dewight replied. "But I need to call fool ass, ASAP" Dewight added. "Yeah, get on that!" Kutta replied.

Dewight picked up his phone and dialed his connect number and waited for him to pick up. He ended the call and dialed the number again and waited once more. When he didn't get an answer the second time, Dewight ended the call and put his phone back down on his lap. He knew when he didn't answer after the second call he wasn't around. "Man, my nigga, this nigga ain't even answering the phone" Dewight said as he drove down East Washington. "Shit, what about shorty?" Kutta asked. "Shorty who?" Dewight replied. "The one we got that last move from, that shit was decent, all my people was fucking with it" Kutta said. "Oh, damn, I forgot about her. I'm finny hit her and see if she got some more of that shit" Dewight said as he picked his phone up and dialed Cocoa's number.

Meanwhile

"I can't leave em alone, tried to change my ways but the dope boys keep turning me on, trap niggas know what I want, I'm so caught up I can't leave em alone…"

"Leave Em Alone" by Layton Greene, Lil Baby, City Girls, and PnB Rock played in the background as Cocoa danced behind Scooter. Scooter stood at the kitchen counter breaking a brick down into hundred-gram portions. Cocoa's phone started to ring, which caused her to stop dancing and take off running into the living room. When she got into the living room, she picked up her phone and noticed it was Dewight's number. "Hey, how are you?" Cocoa asked as she answered the phone. *I'm good, how you been?* Dewight asked. "I been doing fine. What's going on?" Cocoa asked. *Shit, I'm trying to see what's good on your end*, Dewight replied. "Everything is good on my end, if you wanna come down and talk to me" Cocoa said. *It's the same ticket?* Dewight asked. "Well, no, not really, but for you it could be" Cocoa replied. *Ight, well, get a whole demo ready for me, then. I'll be down that way in about an hour*, Dewight said. "Okay, just call me when you make it in town" Cocoa replied. *Tight* Dewight said. "Okay, see you soon" Cocoa replied before she ended the call.

Cocoa placed her phone back down on the coffee table and walked over to the kitchen where Scooter stood and leaned up against the counter next to him and looked at him. "I got some of my people coming down here. Now, I know you're planning on re-rocking most of this shit, but they not going to buy it like that and I wanna keep them around. I be selling them a hundred grams for seven thousand dollars, but they want they whole thing for seventy thousand dollars. I see it as a quick ten thousand if we sell them one" Cocoa said. Scooter stood there nodding his head 'cause he agreed with Cocoa, a ten thousand profit the fast way was good money. "Ight, we can do that." Scooter said before he glanced up at Cocoa, then looked back down at the scale. "I'm going to introduce you to them when they get here and let them know that they can deal with you from here on out" Cocoa said. "Ight, I'm with that. But how long you been fucking wit these niggas?" Scooter asked. "Well, I been knowing him for a few years, but this will be the second time I'm doing business with him" Cocoa said. "Oh, so you trust him?" Scooter asked. "I only asked 'cause I just got out and I ain't tryna go back" Scooter added before Cocoa could reply. "Yes, I trust him! I won't sell it to him if you don't want to" Cocoa said. "Now, naw, I got it. I trust you, so if you trust them, then we good. Plus, I don't want you having to deal with this shit" Scooter replied.

Scooter and Cocoa both looked up at each other when they heard the door be ring. "Who is that?" Scooter nervously asked. "I don't know—oh yeah, as a matter of a fact I do, that's Marsai, I forgot I told her to come over" Cocoa replied. "Ight, just keep her in the living room, I don't want her all in our business" Scooter said. "Alright, I will take her upstairs until you're done" Cocoa said as she walked out of the kitchen and through the living room to the front door. "Hey, girl!" Cocoa said as she opened the door for Marsai. "Hey how you been?" Marsai asked. "I've been doing good! But how you been girl?" Cocoa asked as she closed and locked the door. "I been maintaining, but girl, I'm running low on cash, so I need to get back to work" Marsai replied. "Well, I posted your ad about thirty minutes ago, so once they know you're back around they'll be blowing me up. In the meantime, girl, I got some money for you to make sure you're good" Cocoa said. "I appreciate it, cause girl, I need it" Marsai replied. "You ain't gotta thank me, you know you my bitch and I always got your back. Let's go upstairs" Cocoa said as she led the way up the stairs.

Scooter picked up his phone and dialed Keimon's number and waited for him to answer as it rang. *What up?* Keimon asked when he answered the phone sounding annoyed. "You good, bro?" Scooter asked as he quickly picked up on Keimon's vibe. *Yeah, I'm good, bro. what up? What you want?* Keimon asked. "Damn, bro, don't transfer yo bad energy on me, I just wanted to see when the wedding day was and if you found out anything else about fool?" Scooter asked. *Bro, on some real shit, we both know you on some hating shit with me and Gab! And why you asking about fool over the phone? What, you on some police shit?* Keimon angrily said. Scooter was caught completely off guard by Keimon's response especially the being on some police shit. "Bitch ass nigga, I ain't never been on no police shit! So don't put that jacket on me! And bitch ass nig—" but before Scooter could finish his sentence, Keimon ended the call. Scooter tossed his phone onto the counter pissed off that Keimon just got down on him like that. Keimon had just made him feel even smaller than he'd been making him feel and Scooter had his mind set on knocking Keimon off that high horse.

Meanwhile

Marguerite, Gabrielle's mom Lauren, Stacey, and Gabrielle all sat in Marguerite's living room looking through different wedding books making wedding plans. "So, Gabrielle, what you thinking as far as the venue? You going inside or outside?" Marguerite asked before she took a sip from her glass of red wine. "Well, I've always dreamt of having an outdoor wedding; like in a park or the beach, but then again... I kind of want to have one indoors. I really don't know, y'all, I'm so confused!" Gabrielle replied with stress in her tone. "Okay, just relax, baby! That's why we're here to help you" Lauren said as she reached over and placed her hand on top of Gabrielle's hand. "I still can't believe you and Keimon are about to get married! I always thought y'all made a cute couple!" Stacey said as she flipped through a book of wedding cakes. "Okay, so let's think colors" Marguerite said. "Well, I was thinking lavender and white" Gabrielle replied. "Okay, that's a good start. Lavender and white is good" Marguerite said. "I think Keimon's mansion in California would be perfect to have an outside wedding. His backyard is beautiful with the view of the hills in the background is fire!" Stacey said. Gabrielle looked over at Stacey. "Yes, I think that would be the perfect place to have it, plus it's big enough to hold everyone. Yes! Thank you, Stacey! That's the perfect place" Gabrielle said. "I agree, that would be the perfect place to have it! I love that view!" Marguerite said. "You love what view?" Keimon asked as he walked into the living room and shocked everyone. "The view at your house in California" Marguerite replied. "Oh, okay!" Keimon said as he walked over to her and gave her a hug. "How you doing today?" Keimon asked Lauren. "I'm doing fine, and you?" Lauren asked. "I'm good!" Keimon replied as leaned in and gave her a hug. "I see y'all in her getting it in! What y'all figure out?" Keimon asked before he gave Gabrielle a kiss. "Oh, my bad, what's good, Stacey?" Keimon asked before anyone could answer his first question. "I'm doing fine" Stacey replied.

Gabrielle picked up a book and handed it to Keimon. "Okay, so far we decided we're going with lavender and white as our colors and we'll have the wedding at the mansion in California in the backyard" Gabrielle said. "So, how many people going to be on the guest list?" Keimon asked. "So far we have about seventy people. I think that's enough people" Gabrielle replied. "Well, that's cool, I'm with whatever you want, I wanna make this day beautiful for you. So, let me know what you need me to do" Keimon said. "Okay, I will" Gabrielle replied. "Well, for now Imma let y'all get back to it! Imma be upstairs if y'all need me" Keimon said and started walking out the living room. "I need to talk to you" Marguerite said as she stood up and followed him out of the living room.

Keimon and Marguerite walked into the kitchen. Keimon walked over to the refrigerator and pulled out a bottled water. "So, what up, ma?" He asked. "I got some good news to share with you. I hired a private investigator to find my son and he found out that his name is Deshawn and that he was adopted by a family in Harvey, Illinois. We're still trying to locate him. We reached out to the family and they said they hadn't heard anything from him since he turned 18. I tried Facebook, but he don't have one. But the private investigator promised me that he'll get to the bottom of it and find him for me. I feel like I'm steps closer to finding him, which actually makes me happy." Marguerite said. "That's good news, he know his name and everything now, so he have a lot to start with, plus that's his profession. I'm sure he'll find him. But if you need me to help with anything, just let me know, ma!" Keimon replied. "I will, baby, I just wanted to share that with you I can't wait to find him!" Marguerite said. "But, I'll let you do what you was about to do. Let me go back in here and help Gabrielle 'cause she don't have a clue what she wants, baby! But I got her!" Marguerite said before she walked up to Keimon and gave him a hug and a kiss on his cheek. "I'm proud of you, son!" Marguerite said. "Thanks, ma! I love you" Keimon replied. "Love you too, son!" Marguerite said before she walked away.

Meanwhile
3:30pm

Dewight made a right turn onto Hackett, drove halfway up the block, made a right turn into Cocoa's driveway, and put his car into park. "You coming in or you finna sit out here?" Dewight asked looking over at Kutta. "I'm going in! You know I'm tryna see that ass! Shit, I might shoot my shot!" Kutta said before he laughed "Bro, you funny as hell!" Dewight said as he laughed and turned the car of and took the keys out the ignition. Kutta opened his door and jumped out of the car, Dewight jumped out of the car and walked up to Cocoa's porch with Kutta steps behind him. Dewight knocked on the door then stood there and waited for Cocoa to answer the door. "Hey, Dewight" Cocoa said as she opened the door. "What's going on" Dewight replied. "Come in" Cocoa said as she stepped to the side to let them in. "Hey, it's Kutta, right?" Cocoa asked. "Yeah. How you doing?" Kutta asked as he stepped into the house behind Dewight. "I'm doing fine. How about you?" Cocoa asked as she closed and locked the door. "I'm good" Kutta replied as he glanced down at Cocoa's ass. "That's good to hear, y'all can follow me to the kitchen" Cocoa said as she walked past them and lead the way to the kitchen. They all walked into the kitchen where Scooter sat at the kitchen table. "So, this is my guy, Scooter, Scooter, this is Dewight and Kutta" Cocoa said as she turned around and looked at Dewight then back to Scooter. "What up" Dewight said. "What's going on" Scooter said then stood up to shake Dewight and Kutta's hand.

Scooter paid more attention to Kutta than Dewight cause the name Kutta struck a nerve and all he could think of was the conversation he had with Keimon. "Okay, so, Dewight, from now on, if you decide you want anything, you can deal directly with Scooter. He's good people" Cocoa said. Dewight stood there for a moment. It was something about Scooter that he didn't like, he just couldn't put his hand on it right away. "Ight!" Dewight said with no real intention on dealing with Scooter again. Right now, he needed this shit, so he went along with it. Scooter walked over to the counter and picked up the brick and handed it to Dewight. Dewight looked at it then handed it to Kutta and allowed him to inspect it. "This the same shit?" Dewight asked as he looked over at Cocoa. "No, it's not the same, but it's good shit." Cocoa replied. "Ight, Imma take your word for it" Dewight said. "It's good shit. Yo people gone fuck with it." Scooter said trying to reassure Dewight that he had no worries. Kutta reached into his pocket and pulled out and handed it over to Dewight letting him know he approved of the work. Dewight pulled out and put it with Kutta's money then handed it to Cocoa. Cocoa handed the money over to Scooter to count. "Let me give you his number" Cocoa said to Dewight. "Ight" Dewight said as he pulled his phone from his pocket. "It's 612-563-7689" Cocoa said. "I'm calling it now" Dewight said as he plugged the number into his phone. Scooter's phone started to ring. "That's my number right there" Dewight said before Scooter looked up at the phone. "I got you" Scooter replied. Kutta and Dewight stood there for a few minutes while Scooter finished counting the money. "We good" Scooter said as he sat the last thousand dollars down on the table. "Good looking, Cocoa" Dewight said before he turned to walked out the kitchen. Kutta stuffed the brick on his waistline, adjusted his .9mm on his hip, then walked out the kitchen. Cocoa walked them to the door and opened it. "Y'all drive safe!" Cocoa said as they walked out. "Thanks, we will" Dewight said. Cocoa closed and locked the door, then walked back into the kitchen with Scooter. "Aye, they from Madison?" Scooter asked trying to see if that was the Kutta Keimon mentioned. "Yeah, they from Madison, why you ask that?" Cocoa asked. "They just looked like I seen them before" Scooter replied.

Dewight and Kutta got in the car, backed out the driveway, and started to drive up Hackett. "Bro, I don't like that nigga"

Dewight said. "Why you say that?" Kutta asked. "I don't know, I couldn't pinpoint it" Dewight replied. "What, you think he the police?" Kutta nervously asked. "Naw, bro, I don't think he on no police shit. I just don't like the nigga" Dewight said. "Yeah, that shit crazy!" Kutta said as he pulled the brick from his waistline and placed it on the passenger side floor. "Let's get this shit back to the town I hate driving with this much shit" Dewight said. "Man, 'cause my nigga, we hot ass a bitch!" Kutta replied before he sat back and turned the radio up.

Chapter Ten

* * * * *

Tick walked into Stacey's apartment and locked the door. He walked towards the back room and found Stacey asleep in bed, so he sat on the edge of the bed next to her and shook her to wake her up. Stacey rolled over and looked up at Tick. "Wake yo ass up!" Tick said as Stacey looked at him confused with sleep still in her eyes. "Boy, it's six o'clock in the morning" Stacey replied. "Yeah, I know but I got some shit for you" Tick said. "What's that?" Stacey asked still half asleep. "I got a location on Kutta!" Tick replied. Stacey woke up giving Tick her full attention. "Okay, I'm listening" Stacey said as she sat up. "Alright, check it out, word on the street is that it was Kutta who killed Keimon's brother. I can drop Kutta's location, but it's gone cost him" Tick said. "What happen to you getting him for me?" Stacey asked. "I am, but I figure why not get some of that money from Keimon and let his people do it. I did my part by figuring where the nigga stay. You know, this shit is business" Tick replied. "Alright, how much you trying to get?" Stacey asked. "Tell him I need two-hundred thousand dollars. I know he got it and it ain't shit to him" Tick replied. "Come on, Tick, I don't think he's going to come off that much for him!" Stacey said. "Look, ask the nigga and see what he say!" Tick demanded. "Alright, I will" Stacey said as she rolled out of bed. "Just call me and let me know what up!" Tick said as he got up from the bed. "I got some shit to do, so I'm finna get up out of here. Tell him he got twenty-four hours to get back at me" Tick said before he walked out of Stacey's room down the hall through the living room and out the front door. Stacey stood there shocked she couldn't believe Tick just broke a promise to her and now was using her.

Meanwhile

Dewight sat on the edge of Jessie's bed as she laid there naked on top of the covers sleeping. He picked up his phone from the floor and started to click on his Facebook app, but his phone started to ring before he could. He noticed it was Tick's number, so he answered it. "What up?" Dewight asked. *Shit, cuz, what you on?* Tick asked. "Nigga, it's 6:30, I just woke up! You up early as hell!" Dewight replied. *Yeah, I know, but the money never sleeps cuz!* Tick said. "Yeah, you right on that! But what's the word, though?" Dewight asked. *Shit, man I'm just trying to link up and kick it*, Tick replied. Dewight's antennae went up 'cause Tick never asked to link up with him on some hanging out shit it was always business. Dewight instantly figured something was wrong. "Everything good, cuz?" he asked. *Damn, my nigga! Something gotta be wrong for me to want to link with you?* Tick asked. "Naw, it just ain't something you do, my nigga!" Dewight replied. *Man, cuz, neither is me being up this early, but today is a good day I got a zip of some exotic. I'm tryna smoke this shit with you*, Tick said. "Ight, Imma hit yo line when I get my shit together." Dewight replied. *Bet!* Tick said. Dewight ended the call, stood up, and put his pants back on.

He walked out the room and into the bathroom to piss and wash his face. He walked back into the room and looked down at Jessie and thought about how sexy she looked lying there naked. He reached down and smacked her on the ass and woke her up. "Aye, wake yo ass up and come lock this door" Dewight said. "You going to make me fuck you up if you slap me on my ass like that again" Jessie said as she rolled over on her back. "Naw, but on some real shit, come lock the door. I'm firma get up out of here" Dewight said. "Alright, Imma get up and lock it in a minute" Jessie said as she stretched then rolled back over onto her stomach. "Ight" Dewight said as he walked out the room. He walked through the living room, to the front door and out of the apartment.

He walked into the hall and pulled his phone from his pocket and dialed Kutta's number. He held the phone to his ear as he walked down the stairs, he waiting for Kutta to answer. Dewight walked out the building and to his car and got in. When Kutta didn't answer, he hung up, called again, and waited for him to answer as he pulled off from in front of Jessie's building. *What up, bro?* Kutta asked when he answered the phone still half asleep. "Man, bro, get yo ass up!" Dewight said. *My nigga, I'm woke!* Kutta lied. "Nigga, I can hear the sleep in yo voice! Where you at, I'm finna pull up on you" Dewight asked. *I ain't even around right now. I'm in Kenosha*, Kutta replied. "Fuck you doing down there?" Dewight asked. *I came down here last night with Tamron and a few of her cousins*, Kutta replied. "Ight, bet, just hit me when you touch back down" Dewight said. *Say no more!* Kutta said before he ended the call. Dewight placed his phone in the cup holder and headed towards his crib so he could shower and get dressed for the day.

Meanwhile

Stacey jumped out of the shower, still a little pissed that Tick promised her he would kill Kutta, but now he's using her to get some money out of Keimon. Stacey unwrapped her towel and sat down on the edge of her bed, she reached over to her nightstand and grabbed her body oil and started to oil her skin. "This nigga really don't give a fuck about me!" Stacey said to herself as she oiled her legs and ass. She got up and walked over to her dresser and pulled out some black laced panties from the drawer and put them on. "I shouldn't even call; I should say fuck his ass!" Stacey said to herself as she pulled a black bra out of the dresser drawer. She walked back over to her nightstand and picked up her oil again and started to rub some on her stomach, breasts, and arms. Stacey put on her bra and walked over to the closet to pulled down a pair of skin-tight Prada blue jeans from a hanger and squeezed her way into them. Stacey walked over to her dresser and looked into the mirror and started to put her hair into a ponytail but stopped when she heard the doorbell ring. She walked out of her room, through the living room over to the intercom. "Who is it?" she asked. "It's me, Gabrielle" Gabrielle replied. Stacey buzzed and unlocked the front door.

Gabrielle walked into the building to Stacey's apartment. "Hey, girl!" Stacey said as Gabrielle walked in. "Hey. You still not ready?" Gabrielle asked. "I'm almost ready, bitch, why you rushing me?" Stacey asked. "'Cause we gotta be there by 8:00 am, and bitch, it's 7:30 already!" Gabrielle said as she sat her purse down on the coffee table then sat down on the couch. "Okay, let me put my hair into a ponytail and put my shirt on and I'll be ready" Stacey said as she walked back to her room. Stacey stood in front of her mirror fixing her hair when she thought about what Tick said. "So, bitch, I got something I wanna talk to you about" Stacey said from her room. "Okay, I'm listening" Gabrielle said as she started to flip through her iPhone. "So, I been fucking on this nigga named Tick, and today he came in here and told me that word on the street is that it was Kutta who killed Keef. You heard anything about that?" Stacey asked. "No, I haven't heard anything about that, but there could be some truth to it" Gabrielle replied. "Well, he wanted me to tell Keimon that he knows where Kutta lives and that he'll tell him where for two-hundred thousand dollars. But I feel some type of way 'cause he know Kutta is the one who killed my brothers and now he trying to use what he know to make some money off it" Stacey said. "Yeah, bitch, he ain't shit! You need to stop fucking with that nigga, 'cause he clearly don't mean you no good" Gabrielle said. "Yeah, I was thinking the same thing. But do you think I should tell Keimon about what he said?" Stacey asked. "I think you should, cause Keimon might know more about what's going on out there than we do" Gabrielle replied. "Yeah, I'm going to call and tell him" Stacey said as she walked out of her room and back into the living room fully dressed holding her clutch purse. "About time!" Gabrielle said when she looked up and seen Stacey. "Don't do me!" Stacey replied as he adjusted her ponytail. Gabrielle got up and walked out of the front door heading down the hall. Stacey locked the door behind them and followed Gabrielle to her BMW X6.

Meanwhile

It was 8:45am Eastern time when Keimon pulled up in front of Waun's house on Alta Vista drive in Yonkers, New York. He put his Lincoln Aviator into park and pulled the keys from the ignition. Keimon jumped out of the truck and walked up the stairs onto Waun's front porch and rang the doorbell. Waun snatched the door open, he had been waiting on Keimon's arrival. "Come in, brother!" Waun said. "What's been up, Waun?" Keimon asked as he walked into Waun's house. "Everything is wonderful!" Waun said as he closed and locked the door. "That's good to hear!" Keimon replied. "Yes, yes. Do you want anything to drink?" Waun asked as he walked by Keimon. "Naw, I'm good!" Keimon said. "Okay, let's step into my office" Waun said. Keimon followed Waun through the house and into Waun's office. "Have a seat" Waun said as he pointed to a chair in front of his desk. Keimon walked over to the chair and sat down. "So, what can I help you with?" Waun asked as he walked around his desk and took a seat. "I wanted to stop by personally to tell you that, after this run, I'm going to retire. I feel with me getting married, I need to get out while I can. I made enough money to be able to sit back and focus on my legal business ventures. I plan on starting a family, having a few kids, then sit back and watch them grow old" Keimon replied. "I understand. But are you sure?" Waun asked. "Yeah, I'm sure" Keimon replied. "Alright, well, I'm going to be frank with you Keimon, my brothers are not going to be happy about this" Waun said. "Yeah, I know that's why I'm coming to you, I need you to talk to them and put in a good word for me. I've always been loyal, and we've made lots of money together. Me retiring don't mean this is the end of our friendship. I figure maybe we could go into business another way" Keimon replied. "Like what?" Waun asked. "I been thinking about starting a hotel chain and with y'all connections and my know-how we can open up a chain of hotels in cities all across the United States and make plenty of money to last a lifetime" Keimon replied.

Waun sat there nodding his head 'cause he liked Keimon's idea, but he also knew his brothers wouldn't like losing the money Keimon brought in off their cocaine business. Waun liked Keimon, even though he didn't like many blacks. Keimon showed that he was trustworthy, loyal, and that he had integrity. "You know what, I like your proposal, so I'll talk to my brothers and put in a good word for you" Waun said. "Man, I appreciate it. All I want is to live a long and prosperous life and raise my kids" Keimon said. "Spoken like a true gentleman, I respect it. So, how long are you in town for?" Waun asked. "I fly back out tonight, I gotta get a few things ready for my wedding day" Keimon replied. "Oh, okay" Waun said. "You and your brothers should come; I would really appreciate it" Keimon said. "When is it?" Waun asked. "It'll be in two weeks, on August 8th at my house in California" Keimon replied. "I'll have to check my schedule and check with my brothers. I'll call and let you know" Waun said.

Keimon's phone started to ring, so he pulled it from his pocket and looked at it. "Excuse me, let me take this"

Keimon said when he seen it was Gabrielle's number. "Go ahead. I'll be back." Waun said as he got up and walked out the room. "What's going on, Gab?" Keimon asked as he answered the phone. *Hey, Keimon, this is Stacey*, Stacey said. "What's going on?" Keimon asked. *Well, it's this nigga I talk to, he saying word on the street is that it was Kutta that did that to Keef. He saying he got Kutta's address and he wants to sell it to you*, Stacey replied. "Hold on, who is this nigga?" Keimon asked. *Tick!* Stacey replied. "You talking 'bout Tick that drive the white BMW?" Keimon asked. *Yeah, that's him*, Stacey replied. "Okay, so what he asking for?" Keimon asked. *Two-hundred thousand*, Stacey replied.

Keimon instantly started laughing 'cause he couldn't believe what she just said, but his hatred for Kutta ran so deep there wasn't a price he wasn't willing to pay to see him bleed. "Look, tell that nigga Imma be in town tonight. I wanna meet him face to face. We can talk prices and shit then" Keimon replied. *Alright, I'll do that*, Stacey replied. "Where Gab at?" Keimon asked. *She in there trying on wedding dresses with her mom*, Stacey replied. "Ight, tell her Imma call her later" Keimon said. *Alright, I will*, Stacey replied. "Ight." Keimon said, then ended the call. Keimon looked up at the ceiling and took a moment to take in the information Stacey just gave him. He wanted Kutta's head served to him on a silver platter, bad. He knew he needed to get it done soon 'cause he had plans on living life peacefully, but he wouldn't be able to do that until Kutta was no longer breathing.

Meanwhile

It was 10:00 am and Dewight sat on the passenger side of Tick's Dodge Charger rolling up a backwood as he waited on Tick to come back out of the house he had just walked into. He looked up when he noticed a black Tahoe truck drive slowly pass him. He made eye contact with the driver and instantly felt like they were up to no good. Dewight picked up his phone and called Tick. *What's good?* Tick asked as he answered the phone. "Aye it's some niggas out here looking like they finna get on some bullshit. They looking all up in this mafucka like they looking for somebody. You ain't got shit going on with nobody, do you?" Dewight asked. *You good, cuz, you know I don't be out here beefing wit niggas. Let me finish this shit in here, Imma be out there in a second,* Tick said. "Ight, bet." Dewight replied, then ended the call. He looked into the rearview mirror and noticed that the black Tahoe truck was on its way back around. Dewight pulled his .9mm from his hip and placed it under his thigh. Tuck slowly pulled up next to Tick's car as Red looked into the car. "What up?" Dewight said as he looked at Red. "Slow up, skud, back up real quick!" Red quickly said when he read Dewight's lips. Tuck hit the brakes, threw the car in reverse, and backed up next to Tick's car. Red rolled down the window and signaled Dewight to roll down the driver side window. Dewight reached over and rolled the window down. "What you say, skud?" Red asked. "I said what up! Y'all keep looking in here like y'all looking for somebody!" Dewight aggressively said as he looked at Red. "You can be the nigga I'm looking for since you acting tough!" Red said as he gripped on his FN-15 pistol. "Shit, nigga, it's whatever!" Dewight said as he reached under his thigh to grab his .9mm.

Red noticed Dewight was reaching and quickly upped his FN-15 pistol and pointed it out the window at Dewight. "Nigga, fuck you reaching for?" Red asked as he pointed his pistol at Dewight. "Bro, you trippin'! We on a mission right now!" Tuck quickly said as he reached over and pulled on Red's shirt. Dewight froze in his tracks. He knew Red had the ups on him and there was no way he was able to make it out the situation without getting shot if he pulled his pistol from under his leg. "Bitch ass nigga! You lucky I got more pressing business, or I would spray yo ass!" Red said to Dewight before Tuck slowly started pulling off. Just as Tuck and Red drove by, Tick came walking out of his people's house and jumped in the whip. "Was that them niggas in that truck?" Tick asked as he closed the car door. "Yeah, that was them bitch ass niggas, they just upped on me too!" Dewight replied. "For what?" Tick asked. "I think that's them niggas that's looking for Kutta. Pull back up on them niggas, I'm finna fan they ass down" Dewight said. "Cuz, you trippin'. I ain't finna let you shoot out my car and have my shit hot" Tick replied. "You know what, you right!" Dewight said.

Tick's phone started to ring as he pulled off. He looked down and saw it was Stacey, so he hurried and answered it. "What up?" Tick asked. *Hey, so I called him, and he said that he wanna meet up with you tonight to see if what you got to say is worth buying. Then y'all can discuss prices*, Stacey said. "He ain't say what time?" Tick asked. *No, but I'll call you later,* Stacey said in a somewhat irritated tone. "What's wrong?" Tick asked. *Nothing, why you say that?* Stacey replied. "Cause it sounds like you mad or something." Tick said. *No, I'm good. But I gotta go, I'll call you later*, Stacey replied, then she ended the call.

Tick placed his phone on his lap and looked over at Dewight who was smoking on the backwood he rolled. He knew he was finna cross Kutta out and had to make sure he played Dewight close, so he don't get caught up in the crossfire. Tick sat back and turned up Tee Grizzley's song "The Smartest Intro" and continued to drive.

Chapter Eleven

* * * * *

Later that evening

Scooter turned into his driveway after coming from Cocoa's mother's house. After having a long conversation on loyalty, he was in deep thought about Keef and Keimon and how they grew up together. He was battling with himself as to whether or not he should avenge Keef or use his insight on Keimon and have Kutta take him out. Scooter put the car into park, jumped out, and walked up onto the porch. He hated Keimon cause Keimon was everything that he wanted to be, and he had everything he wanted. Scooter unlocked the door and walked into the house closing and locking the door behind him. He walked to the kitchen and grabbed a bottle of Grey Goose that sat on the kitchen counter and walked to the living room taking a seat on the couch. He pulled his phone from his pocket and flipped through his contacts. He stopped when he came across Dewight's number. "Damn, it's crazy where life takes us to" he said to himself, then pulled the cap off the bottle and took a sip from it. "I can't do this shit!" he said to himself then tossed his phone down on the coffee table. He then took big gulp from the bottle. He was really having a battle within himself as to what was more important to him, his loyalty to Keef or his thirst to see Keimon fall below him where he felt he belonged.

Scooter looked over at his phone on the coffee table then picked it up and pressed the call button and waited for Dewight to pick up. *What up?* Dewight asked as he answered the phone. "What's going on" Scooter asked. *Who is this?* Dewight asked. "This Scooter, Cocoa's guy" Scooter replied. *Oh, damn, my bad, I forgot to log the number in! What's good,"* Dewight said. "Aye, look, I got something I wanna holla at Kutta about. It got something to do with Keimon" Scooter said. *Ight, shit, folks right here, hold on… I'm firma put him on* Dewight replied. "Ight" Scooter said. Dewight looked over at Kutta then tossed him the phone. *Who the fuck is this?* Kutta asked Dewight before he got on the phone. *Just see who it is!* Dewight replied. *What up?* Kutta said as he put the phone to his ear. "Aye, this Cocoa's guy. I got a proposition for you" Scooter said. *I'm listening!* Kutta replied. "I got some information that might be of good use to you. You know Keimon, right?" Scooter said. *Yeah, why, what up?* Kutta asked "Well, I know he looking for you and I figure the enemy of my enemy is my friend! I wanna holla at you, but it gotta be in person" Scooter said. *Ight, when you tryna link?* Kutta asked. "First thing in the AM!" Scooter replied. *Ight, call this number in the morning,* Kutta said. "Ight, bet" Scooter said, then ended the call. He took another big gulp from his bottle he thought to himself now that the ball was rolling. There was no turning back, he had no choice but to see it all the way through.

Meanwhile

Tick pulled up to Stacey's apartment complex and jumped out of his Charger. Keimon had called him ten minutes ago and asked him to pull up. Tick walked up to the building door, unlocked it, and walked to Stacey's apartment letting himself in. He walked into the house coming face-to-face with Keimon and T-mac sitting on the couch. "What's good!" Tick said as he closed and locked the door. "Shit! You tell me!" Keimon replied. Tick looked over at Stacey when she walked out of the kitchen then he looked back to Keimon. "Look, I know you looking for Kutta, the streets talking. I know were the nigga live. I figured I can help you and you can compensate me for my assistance" Tick replied. "Alright, alright. I feel where you coming from, but how do I know you not trying to feed me some bullshit just to get my money?" Keimon asked. "You don't! But you can ask Stacey to vouch that I'm not out here fucked up and in desperate need of money. I ain't known to be no bad businessman and this is business! I stick to my end of business, always" Tick replied. "So, Stacey, what you say?" Keimon asked as he looked at her. "I don't think he's on bullshit. Plus, I'll vouch that he sticks to his word when he's doing business" Stacey said as she looked over at Keimon. Keimon glanced back over to Tick and nodded his head. "Okay, she say you want two-hundred thousand dollars. What makes you think his address is worth two-hundred thousand dollars?" Keimon asked. "Well, me being me, if any nigga kill my brother, it wouldn't be a price I wouldn't pay to get my revenge" Tick replied. "Ight, check it out, you gone swing us by the nigga crib so we can check it out and then I'll give you twenty grand up front, and when I verify that's

129

where he live, then I'll drop off the rest" Keimon said. "Naw, we ain't gone do that. When I give you the info you gone pay me in full, then after the cash is secure, I'll swing you by there so y'all can scope the scene" Tick said. "Fool, you driving a hard bargain!" Keimon replied. "I ain't survive out her this long by being a fool. Who's to say you won't cross me after I give you what you want?" Tick asked. "Just like you, I'm an excellent businessman, I ain't get where I'm at today by doing shady business. But Imma do it yo way cause the more time we go back and forth the more time is wasted. Meet me back here in two hours and we going to swing by his crib. I'll have yo cash right there, but if you play me, I'll put twice as much on your head" Keimon said then stood up from the couch. "Ight, bet" Tick said before Keimon and T-mac walked over to the door and walked out of the apartment.

Four Hours Later

Kutta sat in his living room waiting on E.A. to pull up on him so they could slide on some bitches that E.A. had online. Kutta walked to the window and looked out to see if E.A. pulled into the parking lot yet. He walked back to the kitchen and grabbed a bottle of water because he had popped an ecstasy pill and was rolling hard. He walked back to the window and looked out again before he took a sip from his bottle of water. He then pulled his pistol from his waistline and checked to make sure he had one up top. Just as he tucked his pistol back in his pants, his phone started to ring. He looked down and seen it was E.A. and answered. "Where yo weak ass at?" Kutta asked. E.A. instantly started laughing before he spoke. *On BD, boy, you thirsty as hell. I'm finna pull up come outside!* E.A. replied. "Ight" Kutta said, then he ended the call. Kutta cut off the light and walked out the apartment, locking the door behind him. He rushed downstairs and out the building. He walked into the back-parking lot and looked around for E.A.'s car. He stood there and waited in the parking lot for about five minutes before he started to think E.A. was on bullshit. "Man, this nigga trippin'!" he said as he walked to the edge of the building looking towards the street to see if he could see E.A.'s car. Just as he was about to turn around, he felt cold steel press up against the back of his neck. "Bitch ass nigga, let me see yo hands!" T-mac said as he grabbed the back of Kutta's shirt. "Damn!" Kutta said as he knew he was a dead man. He put his hands up trying to buy as much time as possible and hopes of being able to figure out a way to get the situation. T-mac reached around and patted Kutta's waist and pulled his pistol off his hip. "Yeah, I been waiting to catch yo bitch ass!" T-mac said as he tucked Kutta's pistol in his waist. Tuck quickly pulled from the next parking lot and stopped next to them. Red jumped out of the back of the truck and pointed his FN-15 at Kutta. "Put his bitch ass in the back!" Red said to T-mac. "Naw, y'all gone have to do me right here!" Kutta said knowing if he got into that truck, he was a dead man. "Bitch ass nigga, you finna get yo ass in his car" T-mac said then he smacked Kutta on the top of his head with the butt of the gun. Kutta fell down to one knee and in that moment, he decided to fight and make them do whatever they planned on doing to him right there.

Kutta bounced back to his feet and turned and grabbed T-mac's wrist and pushed him up against the truck, Red rushed over and smacked Kutta in the back of his head with his pistol as he tried to push him into the truck. Kutta wrestled with T-mac over control of his gun as Red tried his hardest not to kill Kutta because Keimon wanted him alive. E.A. pulled into the back lot and seen Kutta wrestling with Red and T-mac, he threw his car into park and hopped out with his .45 and started shooting. His first two shots caught all three of them off guard and dropped Red. Tuck jumped out of the driver seat and fired shots back at E.A. as Kutta continued to wrestle with T-mac. With Kutta being bigger and stronger, he managed to knock T-mac's gun out of his hand then he picked him up and slammed him. He knew T-mac still had his gun, so he took off running through the opposite parking lot. T-mac jumped up and seen Red laying on the ground dead. He ducked behind the truck to take cover from the shots coming from E.A. Tuck ducked from behind the driver's door and returned fire at E.A. before looking over at T-mac who was still ducking behind the truck. E.A. wisely decided, with Kutta being gone, that it was time to get out of there, so he jumped back into his car and backed back out of the parking lot and sped up the street towards Thurston.

E.A. picked up his phone and called Kutta. "Bro where you at?" E.A. asked in a panic as Kutta answered the phone. *I'm on Allied, meet me in the parking lot across from the new buildings*, Kutta replied. "Alright, I'm coming down Thurston now, bro." E.A. said as he sped down Thurston. E.A. made a left turn onto Allied, sped halfway up the block then he made a right turn into the parking lot across the street from the new buildings. He stopped when he seen Kutta standing up against the building holding his t-shirt on the top of his head trying to stop the bleeding. Kutta rushed over to E.A.'s car and jumped into the passenger seat. "Man, my bad, Dave!" E.A. immediately said as he pulled off. He knew it was his fault that Kutta got caught lacking cause he lied about where he was. "I'm good, fool! Pull up to Dewight crib, I need to get something to stop the bleeding, my shit bleeding bad as hell!" Kutta said. "Say no more!" E.A. said and as he headed towards Dewight's crib.

Meanwhile

Tuck couldn't believe shit went the way it just did. He switched lanes and looked back into his rearview mirror to make sure they weren't being followed. "Skud, them bitch ass niggas just killed my cousin!" T-mac said as tears ran down his face. "I can't believe this shit! We need to call that bitch ass nigga Keimon and let him know his change in plans done cost us one of the guys" Tucked said. "This shit ain't on him, bro, we was supposed to have better control over the situation. Naw, fuck what Keimon talking about! I'm killing that nigga myself!" T-mac responded before he picked up his burner phone and called Keimon's number and waited for him to answer.

Keimon heard his burner phone ringing and eagerly jumped out the bed and rushed over to his phone and answered it. "What's good?" Keimon happily asked hoping that he was about hear that they had Kutta. "Man, big bro, shit went all bad! They got Red and the nigga got away!" T-mac exclaimed. "What the hell you mean they got Red?" Keimon asked. "Shit, they killed bro, nigga!" T-mac angrily answered. "Damn! This shit about to be hot! Look, Imma give y'all the bread for his funeral and hit y'all with another ten bands and send y'all back to the city tonight. I'm finna come link up with y'all right now" Keimon said. "Look, bro, them niggas just killed my blood cousin! I ain't going nowhere! I'm about to flip this city upside down! Put a bullet in any and everybody that fuck with that nigga!" T-mac said making sure Keimon knew he was no longer in charge of what was about to happen. "Look, bro, I'm about to link you wit y'all" Keimon said. "Ight, skud!" T-mac said then ended the call.

Keimon sat his phone down and looked over at Gabrielle who laid in bed next to him. "What's wrong?" Gabrielle asked. "This bitch ass nigga, Kutta! He keep getting away. He just killed one of my lil niggas, I gotta take care of this nigga myself. I'll be back in a few hours" Keimon said as he got out of bed and slipped into a pair of sweatpants and left out the room.

The Next Morning

Tick rolled over and looked at Stacey who was still asleep. He was happy that she played her role well. There were a few more things he needed her to do and in due time he would be running the city. Tick looked over at the nightstand when he heard Stacey's phone ring. "Aye, Stacey! Stacey yo phone ringing! "Tick said as he shook her to wake her up. Stacey looked up at him then rolled over and grabbed her phone off the nightstand. "Hello?" She asked as she answered. *Hey, girl! You still sleep?* Gabrielle asked. "I was, but I'm up now. What's wrong?" Stacey asked. *Girl, Kutta is what's wrong,* Gabrielle said. "What you mean?" Stacey asked. *Girl, it didn't go as planned and he killed one of those boys*, Gabrielle said. Stacey sat up in the bed pissed that she just heard that Kutta got away, but Stacey was really mad at Tick 'cause he didn't go along with her plan. She knew Keimon's people wouldn't handle it the way it needed to be handled. "So, he got away?" Stacey asked for more clarification. *Yes! Where are you? I'm about to come meet you so we can talk in person*, Gabrielle asked. "I'm in the room right now, but you can meet me at my house" Stacey said. *Alright, so how long until you get there? I'm about to leave Marguerite house now*, Gabrielle said. "I'll meet you over there in about twenty minutes" Stacey said. "*Okay, girl, see you then*, Gabrielle said. "Okay" Stacey said, then ended the call.

Stacey looked over at Tick and shook her head. She was mad and blamed him for what was going wrong right now. "What's wrong, why you shaking yo head at me?" Tick asked. "'Cause if you would have just listened to me, Kutta would be dead right now" Stacey said. "What you saying they didn't get him?" Tick asked. "Yes, Tick! You should have just got that motherfucker for me! I knew Keimon wouldn't take care of it right" Stacey said. "Look we got two-hundred thousand dollars out the deal, so don't trip. I'm still going to handle it. I just gotta switch a few things up, but in the end, Imma get him. You just make sure you don't steer away from what I told you to do, alright!" Tick said. "I'm not going to go away from the plan, but you better make sure you get him before it's all said and done" Stacey said. "I won't! Trust me" Tick said before he leaned over and kissed Stacey. Stacey was a sucker for Tick, and he knew it, but she loved him and couldn't help but to be just that.

Meanwhile

Dewight pulled up into Cocoa's driveway and put his car into park. He and Kutta both jumped out and walked up to Cocoa's door and rang the doorbell. Scooter looked out the peephole and opened the door. "What's going on?" Scooter asked. "Shit, really!" Dewight said as he walked into the house. Kutta walked in behind Dewight and didn't say anything cause his head banging from the headache T-mac gave him. "You good, bro?" Scooter asked as he noticed the look on Kutta's face. "Yeah, I'm good!" Kutta replied as Scooter closed the door. "But what you wanna holla at me about?" Kutta added as he stood by the door. "Yeah, about that. I know the nigga Keimon. I grew up with him and Keef. He told me that you was the one who killed Keef, but what happened to Keef is between y'all, I ain't got shit to do with that. I do think it's time to get the nigga Keimon out the way and I figured you could help me help you" Scooter said. "Alright! So how you finna help me?" Kutta asked as he stood there looking at Scooter. "Well, I know that the nigga about to get married. Shorty he about to marry live in Madison. I can get her location then y'all can kidnap the bitch. He'll do whatever for her, and y'all having her will draw him out into the open and that's when you get him" Scooter said.

Dewight stood there shaking his head as he took in what Scooter was saying. He couldn't hear past the bad feeling he had about Scooter, it was something he just couldn't pinpoint it, but he felt he needed to fast. "Alright, just call us and let us know what her location is when you find it out and we'll take it from there" Dewight said as he looked over at Kutta, giving him a look letting him know he was ready to get up out of there. Kutta looked at Dewight and caught his drift then looked at Scooter. "Yeah, bro, just call me, Imma be on deck. I gotta get back down here. Imma hit yo line tomorrow though Imma need one more of them demos from you" Kutta said. "Ight, bro, just call me, I got it on deck for you" Scooter replied. "Ight, bro!" Dewight said as he opened the door and walked out. Kutta followed Dewight out the house. They both hopped in the car and briefly chopped it up before pulling off. "Bro, on the G, it's something about this nigga I don't trust" Dewight said as he looked over at Kutta. "I ain't caught that yet! I do know tomorrow we need to re-up. Should we not grab the move from the nigga or not?" Kutta asked. "I don't know! I just don't trust that nigga. We already bought a brick from the nigga, so if he not right he already got us!" Dewight said as he started the car then backed out of the driveway.

Chapter Twelve

* * * * *

Three days later

Cocoa rolled over and looked at her phone when she heard the front door open; it was Scooter walking into the house. She noticed it was 3:00 am and became steaming hot with anger after calling him over nine times and still getting no answer. She couldn't wait until he made his way into the room. Scooter walked up to the bedroom and kicked his shoes off. Cocoa laid there acting as if she was asleep when she noticed Scooter trying to sneak around the room. Scooter walked over to the nightstand on his side of the bed and sat his phones down. He then walked over to the dresser and opened the drawer. Cocoa quickly rolled over when she realized he was about to get in the shower. "So, what bitch got you not answering the phone for me, Scooter?" Cocoa asked. Scooter jumped because Cocoa's sudden outburst startled him. "Damn! You just scared the shit out of me!" he said. "Yeah, I know cause your ass being sneaky!" Cocoa said as she sat up in her bed. "I ain't being sneaky, I just didn't want to wake you up" Scooter replied "Yeah, whatever! But I see you avoided my question!" Cocoa said. "What question was that?" Scooter asked. "See this the shit I'm talking about.

Don't play dumb! You know what, you can go back and spend the night with that bitch!" Cocoa said as she laid back down. "Man, I wasn't with no bitch!" Scooter exclaimed. "Yeah, okay, good night, Scooter" Cocoa said as she rolled her eyes. Scooter walked over to the edge of the bed and sat down next to Cocoa. "Man, you know I love you!" he said as he leaned in and kissed her on the cheek. "Get off me!" Cocoa said as she pushed him away. "Damn, that's how you do me?" Scooter asked. "How I do you? You just avoided nine calls of mine. Then you come in here late! Now you trying to shower and have the audacity to say, "this how you do me?" Look at how you did me!" Cocoa exclaimed. She looked up at Scooter and noticed he'd been crying. "What's wrong?" she added before he had the chance to respond to what she said. "Ain't shit wrong. I'm finna get in this shower" Scooter said, then he got up, grabbed his underwear, and walked into the bathroom.

Cocoa sat up as her mind began to race. She wondered what the hell he was doing out all night. He never stayed out late like that nor avoided her calls, but the dry tear marks on his face is what really had her thinking. She picked up her phone and started flipping through Facebook as she waited on him to get out the shower.

10:30 am

Keimon walked downstairs and found his mother in the kitchen cooking breakfast. "Good morning, ma!" Keimon said as he walked up to her and gave her a hug and a kiss on the forehead. "Good morning, baby! Is Gabrielle up yet?" she asked as she turned back to the stove and started scrambling the eggs again. "Yeah, she up there getting dressed right now. I think she about to go meet up with Stacey and take care of a few things for the wedding" Keimon said. "Well, tell her I made breakfast for all of us. She better not leave until she eat this food!" Marguerite said as she looked back at Keimon. "Alright, I will!" Keimon said as he laughed. "I'm not playing, Keimon!" Marguerite said. "I know, ma, Imma let her know" Keimon said as he reached into the refrigerator and pulled out a jug of orange juice. He walked over to the cabinet and pulled down a glass and poured some juice into it. When he turned around, he seen Gabrielle walking into the kitchen. "Aye, my OG said you can't leave until you eat breakfast!" Keimon said and started laughing. Gabrielle started laughing as well before she looked over at Keimon's mother. "Marguerite, I already know the rules, plus I'm hungry!" Gabrielle said as she walked over to the table and sat down. "I'm happy to hear that you hungry, 'cause I made more than enough for the three of us" Marguerite said as she put the eggs into a bowl and walked it over to the table alongside the other food she cooked.

Gabrielle looked at the bacon, eggs, pancakes, waffles, sausages, diced mixed fruit, and orange juice on the table. "It really is enough food to feed ten people right here, Marguerite!" Gabrielle said. "I know, I over did it!" Marguerite said then she and Keimon both sat down at the table. "Keimon, you wanna say grace?" Marguerite asked. "Yeah, I can!" Keimon said then extended a handout to Gabrielle and his mother and bowed his head. "Lord, we wanna thank you for the many blessings you have bestowed upon us. We come before you today and thank you for providing this wonderful meal. I wanna thank you for giving me a wonderful mother and for giving her the skills to be a great cook. I thank you for blessing me with a beautiful fiancée. We ask you to bless this meal that we are about to partake in, thank you. Amen" Keimon said. "Amen!" Marguerite and Gabrielle both said.

Marguerite reached to the table and grabbed the plate of waffles and placed two on her plate. "So, is y'all excited about the wedding day?" Marguerite asked. "Yeah, I'm excited about it. It seem like time went by so fast. It's three days until the wedding and I still have to do a few more things to get ready" Gabrielle said. "Yeah, time flew by, but I can't wait, honestly!" Keimon added. "I'm excited to watch you guys walk down the aisle together, it'll be a proud moment for me" Marguerite said before her phone started to ring. She looked over at the counter where her phone was then got up from her seat to answer it. "Hey, Charles! How are you?" Marguerite asked as she answered the phone. *I'm doing great! How are you?* Charles asked. "I'm doing good, but I would be doing great if you have some good news for me today" Marguerite said. *Well, I do have some good news for you! I found your son and you're not going to believe this, he's in Madison. I talked to his girlfriend today. I don't have an address or number for him yet. However, I do have a picture of him for you. I'm waiting on his girlfriend to get back to me after she makes sure it's okay with him for her to give me his number. I'm sending the picture over now and I'll call you as soon as I get his phone number*" Charles said. "Alright, Charles and thank you so much!" Marguerite replied. *No problem, enjoy your good news!* Charles said. "Thank you! And you enjoy your day as well!" Marguerite said, then ended the call. She walked back over to the table and sat back down.

Keimon looked over at his mother and seen she was smiling ear to ear. "You smiling super hard over there, what you got going on?" Keimon asked. "I have some great news! My private investigator found Deshawn and he lives here in Madison. He got in contact with his girlfriend and talked to her. Now he's waiting for her to get back to him with his number" Marguerite said as she smiled from ear to ear. "That's what's up!" Keimon said. "Yes, it is! I wonder if we know him!" Gabrielle added. Marguerite's phone chimed with a text from Charles, so she quickly clicked on the text and opened it. "Oh my God, my son look just like me!" Marguerite said as she studied Deshawn's features. "Let me check it out!" Keimon said as he got up from his seat and walked over to where is mother was sitting and looked over her shoulder at the picture. Marguerite looked over her shoulder at Keimon, she was caught off guard by his facial expression. "Do you know him?" Marguerite asked. "No, ma, I don't" Keimon said as he looked over to Gabrielle. Gabrielle got up from her seat and walked over to check the picture out. She looked down at the picture then to Marguerite then over at Keimon. "Do you know him?" Marguerite asked Gabrielle. "No, I don't" Gabrielle said before she walked back over to her seat and sat back down. "Why y'all acting so strange?" Marguerite asked as she looked at Keimon then to Gabrielle. "I gotta a make run! I'll be back!" Keimon said, then he rushed out the kitchen.

Meanwhile

Stacey pulled up to Marguerite's house and pulled out her phone and dialed Gabrielle's number. She was in a great mood 'cause things had been going good between her and Tick. She finally had his full attention, which was just what she wanted. "Hello?" Gabrielle asked as she answered the phone. *Girl, I'm outside!* Stacey exclaimed. "Okay, here I come now" Gabrielle said, then ended the call. Stacey danced in her seat to Toosii's "Love Cycle Remix" featuring Summer Walker as she waited on Gabrielle. Gabrielle walked out of Marguerite's house a few minutes later and started laughing when she seen Stacey with her head down rocking dancing in her seat.

Gabrielle walked up to the car and opened the door. Stacey looked up and started laughing herself before she turned the music down. "Bitch, you in love? You in here in a zone" Gabrielle said as she got into the car and closed the door. "No, I'm not in love, I just feel good today" Stacey said as she put the car into drive and pulled away from Marguerite's house. "Girl, I don't wanna piss in your corn flakes, but I found out some fucked up shit this morning" Gabrielle said. "I don't wanna hear no bad news, I'm in a good mood" Stacey said as she looked over at Gabrielle then back to the road. "Trust me, you wanna know this!" Gabrielle said. "Bitch, I'm just going to go ahead and say it. Keimon and Kutta are brothers!" Gabrielle added. Stacey looked over at Gabrielle and started laughing. "Bitch, you play too much!" Stacey said as she continued to laugh. "No, I swear I'm not playing with you. Marguerite had a private investigator look for her son that she gave up for adoption at birth in Chicago when she was younger. Well, bitch, he found him, and the motherfucker is Kutta! The investigator sent a picture to Marguerite's phone today and I swear to you it was Kutta! Keimon acted like he didn't know him and rushed out the house. He hasn't been answering my calls or anything" Gabrielle said in a serious tone. Stacey looked over at her and seen the seriousness in Gabrielle's eyes which blew her fucking mood. "This is some trippy shit! I can't believe this! I'm telling you now, I don't care how Keimon feels about this shit, but Kutta still has to die! He killed my fucking brothers!" Stacey angrily said as she continued to drive. "I think he deserves to die after what he did to your brothers and Keef. But Keimon is about to be my husband and I have to side with him with whatever he decide to do" Gabrielle said. "Well, he's not about to be my husband, and his brother or not, Kutta going to get what's coming to him" Stacey said as she slowed down and stopped at the red light. "I'm not about to argue with you" Gabrielle said with an attitude. "Good, 'cause I'm a grown ass woman and I'll do whatever I please" Stacey said. "Okay, bitch, whatever" Gabrielle said then turned the music up, so she didn't have to listen to shit else Stacey had to say about the situation.

Three o'clock

Cocoa needed someone to vent to, so she and Marsai sat in at Longhorn Steakhouse on State Street. in Rockford, Illinois enjoying a late lunch. "Girl, I don't know what to think. Scooter was acting real strange last night. He avoided answering my calls all night, then he came in the house late, and jumped into the shower. Something's not right" Cocoa said before she took a bite from her steak. "Has he ever done this before?" Marsai asked. "No, he's never missed a call and he always come home at a reasonable time. I noticed he had tear marks on his face which told me he had been crying, but when I asked him about it, he avoided answering the question" Cocoa said as she began to think back on what happened. "You know I don't do relationships, so I'm not good on giving advice about it" Marsai said as she took a bite of her salad. "Girl, I know, I just need somebody to be right here while I talk so I don't look crazy. I'll think myself through the situation" Cocoa said.

Just then, her phone started to ring in her purse. She reached in and pulled it out and looked at it and seen that it was Shauri. Shauri is Cocoa's younger cousin. Cocoa introduced Shauri's boyfriend, Justin, to Scooter. Justin was a true hustler who needed connections and she figured they could capitalize off his grind. "Hey, Shauri, what's going on?" Cocoa asked. *That's what y'all on?* Justin asked. "What you mean?" Cocoa asked confused because Justin never called off Shauri's phone. *Yo nigga just tried to set me up!* Justin said. "Hold on, wait! What?" Cocoa asked not sure if she heard him right. *Man, look, Cocoa, you linked me in with this nigga, so I hold you responsible!* Justin said, then ended the call. "Hello? Hello?" Cocoa said, then looked to the phone and realized Justin hung up.

Cocoa's mind quickly began to race with thoughts as she wondered what the hell Justin meant by holding her responsible. She had no clue what the hell was going on. She dialed Scooter's number and waited for him to answer so she could get to the bottom of this shit, but the phone went unanswered. She immediately called back, but this time, she was sent straight to the voicemail. Cocoa placed her phone down on the table and looked over at Marsai. "You okay?" Marsai asked. "No, this nigga is about to stress me out" Cocoa said as she put her hand on her forehead. She loved Scooter dearly, but in the pit of her stomach, she knew something wasn't right.

Meanwhile

Gabrielle and Stacey walked into Gabrielle's duplex on Church Hill after running the last errands for her wedding day. Stacey walked into the kitchen and sat the leftovers from their lunch on the kitchen counter. Gabrielle walked upstairs to gather a few things so she could be ready for her flight to California tonight. Stacey walked back into the living room, and looked out the window, then walked upstairs to Gabrielle's room and stood in the doorway. "What time is your flight tonight?" Stacey asked. "We fly out at 9:00 pm. I can't wait until this wedding is over and I can sit back and relax. I been running around like crazy; I should have hired a wedding planner. I know I need to figure out what I'm about to do with my time now that Keimon don't want me handling the business down here" Gabrielle said. "So, what is he going to do about that? I do depend on that money and could use that job" Stacey said. "I'm not sure, we haven't really had time to sit down and talk about it. I can put in a good word to him about letting you run things" Gabrielle said. "I don't think he'll let me handle it cause of what happened with Kutta" Stacey said before her phone started to ring. She had been waiting on Tick to call and give her the go ahead on their next move. "Hold on, let me take this call" Stacey said as she walked out the room. "Okay" Gabrielle said as she looked back at Stacey as she walked out the room. "Hello" Stacey whispered as she answered. *They outside right now!* Tick said. "Okay" Stacey said. She walked down the stairs and to the front door and opened it, she looked at Kutta, then to Dewight. "She's upstairs" she said as walked out the house to her car, preparing to leave the area. "My part is done! Now, you better make sure you get him this time, Tick!" Stacey said as she pulled off. *Look, I got this handled, just meet me at your crib in two hours*, Tick replied. "Alright, I will see you then." Stacey said, then ended the call.

Kutta walked into the house with Dewight steps behind him. Dewight closed and locked the door as Kutta slowly crept up the stairs. "Bitch, you been real secretive lately!" Gabrielle said when she heard the footsteps coming up the stairs. She stuffed her swimsuit into her Gucci suitcase and started folding a pair of shorts. Kutta walked into the bedroom and pulled his .9mm from his waist and pointed it at Gabrielle. "Bitch, where you finna go?" Kutta asked. Gabrielle quickly turned around when she seen Kutta the shock and fear caused her to drop to her knees. "Kutta, please!" she begged as she struggled to breathe. Kutta laughed as he walked over to her and grabbed her by the hair and pushed her down on her stomach. "If you get loud, I'll kill you! You understand?" Kutta asked. "Yes! I understand! I won't! Just please, don't hurt me!" Gabrielle said. "I promise I ain't gone hurt you!" Dewight said as he walked further into the room. "But you gotta do something for me in return!" Dewight said. "What?" Gabrielle nervously asked as she looked around for Stacey. "Get Keimon to come over here" Kutta replied. Gabrielle put her head down out of fear and in shame, she didn't want to set her fiancé up, but she knew she needed to buy herself some time. "Okay! Okay! I will get him to come over" Gabrielle said. "Where the fuck is yo phone?" Dewight asked. "It's over on the dresser in my purse!" Gabrielle said as she laid on the floor. Dewight walked over to the dresser and looked inside Gabrielle's purse to pull out her phone. "You finna call this nigga and make it seem like it's an emergency to get him over here! If you tip him off, I'm going to have to go back on my word and kill you! Trust me, I don't like to go back on my word. So, be a good girl and do as you're told, Okay?" Dewight said. "Alright! I will do whatever you say, just please, don't hurt me." Gabrielle said.

Kutta sat down on Gabrielle's bed and looked down at her as she laid on the floor. "You really gotta pick your friends more wisely 'cause Stacey really wasn't a good one. You know she set this up, she was pissed at you and Keimon for getting her brothers killed. But don't worry, she'll get hers" Kutta said then started laughing. Dewight looked at Kutta and shook his head letting him know he needed to stop talking 'cause she hadn't called Keimon yet. Kutta nodded his head, then put his hand over his mouth. "Bitch, get up!" Kutta angrily said as he reached down and pulled Gabrielle up to her feet. "Y'all getting married soon, huh?" Kutta asked. "Yes" Gabrielle replied. "Okay, call him and tell him you're getting cold feet and you not sure if you want to marry him. Tell him you need him to come over and talk to you, ASAP." Kutta said. "Okay" Gabrielle said.

Dewight walked over to the bed and handed Gabrielle the phone. "Put the phone on speaker, I wanna hear everything!"

Dewight ordered. Gabrielle scrolled through her contacts and found Keimon's number and called him. Dewight and Kutta both stood there listening as the phone rang. "What up, Gab?" Keimon asked as he answered the phone. "Hey, I need to see you" Gabrielle sadly said. "What's wrong?" Keimon asked when he heard the stress in her tone. "I don't think I'm ready!" Gabrielle replied. "So, what you saying? You not ready to get married?" Keimon asked. "Yes, Keimon! I'm getting cold feet! I need you to come over here as soon as possible! I need to look you in your eyes so you can reassure me that this is what's best for us both. I need to know before we get on this flight tonight!" Gabrielle said as she started to cry 'cause she knew she was calling Keimon to his death. "Man, don't cry! Where you at?" Keimon asked. "I'm at home!" Gabrielle said as she continued to cry. "I'm on my way over there now, give me like fifteen minutes" Keimon replied. "Alright" Gabrielle said, then she ended the call. Dewight snatched the phone from her hands and looked over at Kutta. "Alright, now tie this bitch up!" Dewight said to Kutta. Without any hesitation Kutta went to work. He snatched the sheets from the bed, ripped them into pieces, then tied Gabrielle up. Tick sat low in his car six buildings down from Gabrielle's duplex and watched as Keimon pulled up in his Cadillac truck and jumped out. He was extremely excited cause his plan was coming to fruition.

Keimon walked up to the door and put his key into the lock opening the door. He walked in and looked around. "Aye, Gab!" Keimon called out as he looked around. He entered and walked into the living room. He stopped in his tracks when he found Dewight sitting on the couch pointing his gun at him. "Come on over here and sit down real quick!"

Dewight said. Keimon took a step back when he noticed the gun in Dewight's hand. "Bitch ass nigga, go have a seat!" Kutta said from behind Keimon before he pressed his pistol to the back of his head. Keimon put his hands up as piss began to run down his legs. "Aye, Kutta, look, bro... don't do this shit!" Keimon said. "Bitch ass nigga, we ain't cool! Don't call me bro!" Kutta said as he pushed Keimon into the living room. Kutta walked up and patted Keimon down to make sure he didn't have a gun on him "Folks, this bitch ass nigga pissed on himself!" Kutta said and started laughing. "Look, man! I called my niggas off today when I found out that you really my brother! Our mother was forced to give you up for adoption when she was younger!" Keimon said. "Bitch ass nigga, you ain't my blood!" Kutta shouted, then smacked Keimon in the back of his head with his pistol knocking him to the floor. Keimon balled up and covered his head as he hit the ground. "Bro! I ain't lying! Yo real name is Deshawn, you grew up in Harvey and you ain't seen your foster parents since you was 18 years old! How would I know any of that shit if it wasn't true!" Keimon said as he tried to beg Kutta not to do what he was about to do.

Kutta looked over at Keimon shocked that he knew so much shit about him, but he still didn't believe a word he said. He walked over to Keimon and kicked him in his stomach. "Bitch ass nigga! Shut the fuck up! You tried to get me killed twice! But every time I survived that shit! Now I got the upper hand on you and I'm finna make sure you don't survive what I'm about to do to you" Kutta said as he walked over to Keimon and pointed his pistol down at him. "Go get that bitch!" Kutta demanded Dewight. Dewight jumped up from the couch and rushed up the stairs and dragged

Gabrielle back down the stairs. Keimon looked over and seen Dewight pulling Gabrielle like she was a dog on a leash. "Bro! she ain't got shit to do with this!" Keimon said. "Damn, I seen this movie before!" Kutta said and started laughing. "Your brother said the same shit before I killed his pussy ass" Kutta added. Kutta's comment sent Keimon over the edge. He knew there was no getting through to Kutta and he refused to die like a bitch. Keimon quickly reached up and knocked Kutta's gun out his hand causing it to slide across the wood floor. He jumped up to his feet and picked Kutta up and slammed him into the coffee table. Then jumped on top of him and punched him continuously as Dewight slowly walked over and picked up Kutta's gun. "Folks, you finna let this nigga kick yo ass?" Dewight asked Kutta as he watched Keimon pound away at him. Kutta grabbed ahold of one of Keimon's arms and pulled him close to him then pushed him over onto his side rolling on top him. He punched Keimon a few times before he jumped to his feet and kicked Keimon in his stomach. "Give me my shit!" Kutta said as he turned and snatched his pistol from Dewight then turned back and emptied his clip into Keimon. "Man, what the fuck! Now we gotta hurry up and get the fuck out of here!" Dewight said as he rushed to the window and looked outside. "Give me yo demo!" Kutta said to Dewight. Dewight handed Kutta his pistol then Kutta walked over to Gabrielle and shot her twice in the head. They rushed out the back door and took off running through a backyard to the next street over to their car and peeled off.

Stacey unlocked the door and walked into Keimon's stash house with Tick steps behind her. Tick entered and locked the door behind him. He was taken aback by the layout of the spot as he looked around the house. The spot didn't look like your average stash house; it was elegant and looked as if someone lived there. "You know where that shit at?" Tick asked. "Yeah, I do, but before I go get it, I need you to tell me the rest of the plan 'cause you still haven't killed Kutta" Stacey said. "Come on now, Stacey, you tripping! But since you need to know so bad, I got plans to meet with Kutta and Dewight so I can cut them in on what I get out of here! That's when I'll kill both of them myself" Tick said. Stacey looked at him as she tried to judge if he was telling her the truth. "I wanna be there so I can watch him die!" Stacey said. "Man, go get the shit, you know damn well you ain't never seen nobody die, so why the hell you tryna see some shit now?" Tick asked. "Because he killed my fucking brothers! I could have killed him today, but I'm following your fucking lead which is starting to make me feel like you playing on my feelings for you!" Stacey angrily said as she stood there with her hands on her hips looking at Tick. "Stacey, we ain't got all night! Now go and get the shit so we can go meet these niggas! Since you wanna watch you might as well kill him yourself with yo tough ass!" Tick said. "You know what, fuck you, Tick!" Stacey said as she walked away. Tick followed her to a room upstairs and watched as she walked over to the bed and looked under it pulling out a black duffle bag, then looked back at him. "You happy now?" Stacey asked after she unzipped the duffle bag so Tick could see what was in it. Tick walked over and looked into the bag and his eyes became buck wide when he seen it was stuffed with bricks of cocaine. He knew he hit the jackpot. "Yeah, I am happy now!" Tick said then he looked over at Stacey and pulled out his pistol and shot her in the chest. She dropped to the floor. Tick walked closer and stood over her to say a few last words. "Bitch, you crossed your best friend and the nigga that been feeding you for years. You honestly think I was gone trust you after that? Bitch, tell Satan I'll see him when it's my turn!" Tick said before he shot Stacey three more times. He quickly zipped up the duffle bag and casually walked out the room.

Chapter Thirteen

* * * * *

C ocoa laid in bed watching TV when her phone started to ring. She reached over and grabbed it off the nightstand. She looked over and seen that it was Dewight's number, so she answered it. "Hello?" Cocoa said as she answered. *Aye, Cocoa, tell me you ain't have nothing to do with that shit...* Dewight said. "What happened?" Cocoa asked concerned. *Yo nigga just set folks up!* Dewight answered. Cocoa put her head down in shame before she responded. It all now made sense why Scooter had been acting so strange, coming in at weird hours of the night, and some nights not coming home at all. "Dewight, I swear, I didn't have anything to do with any of that. I haven't heard from him in two days now. I would never intentionally put you in harm's way, I have too much respect for you and your father. But I promise you, I'll take care of it, Dewight" Cocoa said. *Yeah, do that* Dewight said, then ended the call.

Cocoa sat there in disbelief. She was deeply in love with Scooter and now hearing that he's working with the police destroyed both her and her image. She dialed Scooter's number and waited for him to answer. *What up, beautiful?* Scooter asked as he answered the phone. Cocoa rolled her eyes at his comment before she spoke. "Scooter, why haven't I heard from you in the past two days?" she asked. *Baby, I had to take a trip and take care of some shit. I turned my phone off and I couldn't make no calls 'cause I didn't want my phone to ring. But I'll be home tonight, I promise*, Scooter replied. "You sure?" Cocoa submissively asked. *Yeah, baby, I promise*, Scooter replied. "Please, don't come in late. I'm tired of sleeping by myself, Scooter" Cocoa said. *I won't, I'll be home by 6:00 pm*, Scooter said. "Alright, 'cause I think we have a few things we really need to talk about" Cocoa said. *Alright, we can do that. But let me finish this shit up and I'll see you when I get home*, Scooter said. "Alright, I love you" Cocoa replied. *Love you, too*, Scooter said, then ended the call. Cocoa sat on the edge of her bed. She hated being in the position of having to choose between her happiness and what she believed to be right.

8:30 pm

Scooter pulled up to Cocoa's house, parked his car, and jumped out. He rushed up onto the porch and unlocked the door then walked into the house. He knew he promised Cocoa that he'd be home by 6:00 pm, so he quickly made his way up the stairs and to her bedroom. He looked around the room and didn't see any sign of her or that she had even been there. "Aye, Cocoa!" Scooter called out to her. "I'm down here in the kitchen!" Cocoa yelled from downstairs. Scooter sat his phone on the dresser and walked downstairs to the kitchen. Cocoa sat at the table eating when Scooter walked into the kitchen. He walked over to her and kissed her on the forehead. "I missed you!" Scooter said. "I missed you too"

Cocoa replied as she avoided making eye contact with him. Scooter peeped her sudden discomfort. "What's wrong?" he asked. "Nothing" Cocoa said as she continued to eat her food. "You don't look like it's nothing, Cocoa" Scooter said as he walked over to the refrigerator and opened it. "You know what, there is something wrong. Answer me this, and please don't lie to me" Cocoa said. "Alright, I won't" Scooter said without hesitation. "I got a call today from Dewight saying that you set Kutta up with the police. Please tell me this nigga is mistaken and this shit is not true, Scooter" Cocoa said. Scooter closed the refrigerator and turned to face Cocoa then leaned up against it. "Look, Cocoa, about a week ago, I got pulled over on my way back from Rockford and I got caught with two bricks. I didn't want to throw away everything that we had, so I made a deal to work with the Feds" Scooter said as he looked at her.

Cocoa instantly pushed her plate across the table, causing it to crash onto the floor. "Scooter, I introduced you to my people and you shit on my name. You could've done that shit to your people." Cocoa seethed, looking at him. "Cocoa, I did! I did this shit for us, fuck all them. It's about you and me" Scooter replied. "No, Scooter you did this shit for yourself! Not once did you ask me what I think about this shit. Scooter, I don't agree with what you did, my last nigga was set up by a pussy ass nigga like you. I swear, I just went from loving you with everything in me to hating your fucking guts all in one breath" Cocoa said as she put her hands over her face. "Damn, it's like that?" Scooter said as he stood there with the stupid look of disbelief on his face. "Yes! Please get your shit and leave" Cocoa said.

Scooter stood there in complete disbelief, but his disbelief turned into panic when Dewight walked into the kitchen. "I'm happy to hear it from your mouth that it was you that jammed folks up!" Dewight said as he pointed his pistol at Scooter. "Damn, Cocoa, this how you do me?!" Scooter asked, panicked, as he looked over at her expecting her to save him. "Nigga, fuck you, I'm done with yo trifling ass. Do what you want with this nigga" Cocoa said to Dewight as she walked past Scooter. "Don't make no mess in my house" Cocoa said as she walked away. "I got you" Dewight said as he walked over to Scooter and grabbed him by his shirt and yanked him out of the kitchen.

Dewight opened the basement door and walked Scooter down into the basement. Scooter noticed he was nearing death and tried to turn and run back upstairs. Dewight cocked back and hit Scooter with a right hook, dropping him to his knees. Dewight grabbed Scooter and dragged him into the basement and pushed him on top of a plastic tarp. "Please man, please!" Scooter begged. Dewight pulled his pistol from his waist and shot Scooter in the face. He made sure he kept his word to Kutta and cut Scooter's life short. Dewight put on a pair of latex gloves and picked up his shell casing, then he started rolling Scooter's body up in the tarp. He dragged him upstairs to the garage and put him in his trunk. Dewight opened the garage door and pulled out slowly, pulling off into the night.

Also Available by Bagz of Money Content

Live by It, Die by It (By: Ice Money)

Mercenary (By: Ice Money)

The Ruler of the Red Ruler (By: Kutta)

Block Boyz (By: Juvi)

Team Savage (By: Ace Boogie)

Team Savage 2 (By: Ace Boogie)

Team Savage III (By: Ace Boogie)

Love Have Mercy (By: Kordarow Moore)

Rich Pride (By M.L. Moore)

Available at Bagzofmoneycontent.com and most major bookstores.

Made in the USA
Coppell, TX
27 February 2024

29517472R00089